THE
Christmas
SCRAMBLE

ALEXIS
BUXTON

Before You Read

This book does feature a few trigger warnings. Please read on with caution as these triggers may be considered spoilers.

This book features the main character suffering a stroke and the first few chapters take place in a hospital setting. The Christmas Scramble is an open-door romance with explicit sexual content, strong language, as well as college-aged main characters drinking. It is my hope that I've handled these topics in the care that they deserve. Readers, please be advised.

Playlist

Make You Mine This Season - Tegan & Sara
How to Save a Life - The Fray
Hallelujah - Pentatonix
By Your Side - Mike Perry
Home - Phillip Phillips
Favorite Time of Year - Carrie Underwood
This Christmas - Maddie & Tae
Take Me Home for Christmas - Dan & Shay
Last Christmas - Wham!
Let It Be Christmas - Alan Jackson
Santa Claus is Coming to Town - Michael Buble
All We Need - Andrew Hyatt
Officially Christmas - Dan & Shay
I Hope It Snows - Mitchell Tenpenny
Sleigh Ride - Brett Eldredge
Santa Claus is Back in Town - Cody Johnson
Wit It This Christmas - Ariana Grande
Christmas in the County - Thomas Rhett
Snow's Not the Only Thing Falling - Patrick Murphy
Christmas Cookies - George Strait
Christmas in Hollis - Run DMC
Santa Tell Me - Ariana Grande
Mistletoe - Justin Beiber
Christmas (Baby Please Come Home) - Chris Young
Shimmy Down the Chimney - Alison Krauss
Christmas Eve - Justin Beiber
All I Want For Christmas Is You - Morgan Evans
Have Yourself a Merry Little Christmas - Michael Buble

For the complete soundtrack, search 'The Christmas Scramble' on Spotify!

To those who love love, keep kissing those toads.
The one is right around the corner.

Chapter 1

"MAYBE I WOULD HAVE SOME KIND OF UNDERSTANDING OF THE MEDICAL FIELD
IF I WAS ONE OF THOSE GIRLS WHO OBSESSED OVER MCDREAMY."

"You need to get to the hospital right now."

Is this some kind of prank?

Pulling the phone away from my ear, I stare at the unknown number. I'm not one to answer a number I don't have, but the local area code has me concerned.

"I'm sorry, but who is this?" I ask the unknown caller. My eyes skirt around my room, a strange feeling washing over me.

Who would pull a prank by calling a random number and telling them to get to the hospital?

"Macy, it's Rick." Silence stretches between the two of us as I can't place the name right away. He must figure out my silence reflects confusion because he quickly clarifies. "Rick, Gregg's friend and teammate. Gregg's in the hospital, and you need to get here *now*."

A small gasp escapes my lips. Gregg is in the hospital? Why is Rick calling me? I mean, I appreciate the call, but we aren't in a relationship. We're just casual, hell, not even that. We're just hooking up. Oh, who am I kidding?

"I-I-I'll be right there!" I stammer, rushing to my closet to find a pair of shoes. Rick ends the call, promising to text me the details on which hospital and where to go. Within five minutes, I'm rushing out of the townhouse. I've never been more grateful that my two roommates aren't home. I don't have time for their mini-interrogations.

The drive from the townhouse to the hospital is quick. Traffic seems to be on my side for once. I'm a blur as I frantically run through the emergency room doors. The smell of antiseptic greets me as the chaos of the emergency room surrounds me. Hospitals aren't something I am familiar with. The only time I've been to one was when I was thirteen and my cousin had her baby. This is nothing like that. Shock and confusion run circles through my brain as I try to figure out why Rick called me. He knows Gregg and I are just having fun together, which makes me worry this is something serious. And with that thought, dread forms like a bowling ball in the pit of my stomach.

"Macy!" I hear my name from my right. Spinning on my toes, I spot some of the players on the golf team, Coach Jones—who everyone just callsCoach, and Rick.

My pace quickens as my pulse pounds and sweat gathers in my palms. The need to wipe my hands on something intensifies as I make my way over to Rick. "What's going on?"

Reaching out, Rick gently takes my arm, tugging me to sit down in a vacant chair next to him. The look on his face is eery and not helping the weight on my chest. "Rick? You're freaking me out."

"Sorry," he says with a sigh, clearing his throat before he continues. "We think Gregg had a stroke."

Oh my gosh.

I can feel the blood drain from my face as shock takes over. "Wh-what do you mean?" I ask, glancing around the waiting room. It's then I notice all the somber expressions and the worried look on the coach's face.

This can't be happening.

"We were out on hole six for our practice. Gregg said that he was getting a migraine, but it was practice. He knew he couldn't just leave. He was lining up for a putt, and that's when I noticed him start to sway. His words were jumbled, and he blinked rapidly when I asked if he was okay." Rick pauses, and I can see the pain on his face as he relives the afternoon.

Reaching out, I grab his hand. With a small squeeze, I give him the comfort to keep going.

"Then suddenly, he just collapsed to his knees on the green, clutching his head. I called Coach, and while he made his way out to us, he called a squad. The paramedics are pretty certain Gregg suffered a stroke, but that's all we know," Rick says, taking a ragged inhale.

"But he's young. Aren't strokes for when you're older?" I ask. I've never wished to be a Grey's Anatomy girl until this point. Maybe I would have some kind of understanding of the medical field if I was one of those girls who obsessed over McDreamy.

Rick shrugs his answer. "I honestly have no clue. Right now, we are just waiting on the doctors. Gregg's parents are out of town, so they gave permission for the doctors to communicate with Coach and, um, Gregg's girlfriend."

My eyes widen at the realization of what Rick just said. "His girlfriend? Oh my God, Gregg has a *girlfriend*?"

A small laugh leaves his lips. "No, Macy. It's you. Gregg must've told them about you, and they assumed that you two were seeing each other. They want you and Coach to be the ones that can see him and listen to any medical jargon."

Chest heaving as the reality sets in, I feel another zap of energy run through my veins.

Gregg had a stroke.

He's talked to his parents about me—his only-supposed-to-be-a-one-time-thing hookup.

And his parents think I'm his girlfriend.

Before I have a chance to spiral, a man in his mid-forties wearing a white jacket approaches our group. "I'm looking for a Mr. Jones and a Macy Miller."

Coach makes eye contact with me, and the two of us stand, making our way to the doctor. "Hello, I'm Doctor Grey, and I'm Gregg Carlton's doctor. Can we step over here to speak in a more private area?"

Following the doctor to a more secluded part of the waiting room, the panic hasn't subsided. If the doctor wants to speak to us in private, there's no way this can be good. And of course this doctor's name is Grey. I might not have been a religious follower of Grey's Anatomy, but I do know that's one of the doctors' names.

"It appears that Gregg has suffered a massive stroke—"

A loud gasp escapes as the shock of the words hit me like a freight train. My knees feel like they could buckle at any moment. Coach Jones reaches down and squeezes my hand. In a normal setting, the extra contact would make me cringe, but right now, I'm in such a state of shock that any and all contact is welcomed. It's grounding, a reminder that I'm not alone and this is real. I'm not dreaming.

"I know this is quite a shock," the doctor continues. "But we have the best of the best here. Upon arrival, we rushed Gregg to an MRI with contrast, but once he finished the test, he began to decline rapidly. He started to show signs of aphasia—"

"Sorry, Doctor, but can you dumb this down?" I ask, not caring that I interrupted the doctor, again.

"Aphasia means he couldn't speak due to brain damage. He also couldn't see."

I think I'm going to pass out. My knees begin to quake, and my chest feels like it could explode. But before I have a chance to react, the doctor continues.

"Right now, we are running an extensive panel of tests to determine where the clot came from. This could be a relatively fast process, or it could take some time. I just wanted to come out for a quick update. I'll be back out when we have more answers."

"Thank you, Doctor," Coach responds, sticking his hand out for the doctor to shake. With a nod, Dr. Grey turns and heads back through the secured doors. Coach leads me back to where the team is waiting for an update. I continue walking over toward the windows and peer out over the parking lot.

I heard the news once; I don't need to hear it again.

Right now, my body is in shock. Gregg is young. He's healthy. How can he be experiencing a stroke?

It's after midnight when Rick finally gets me to leave the hospital. At some point, I had fallen asleep, curled up in a waiting room chair. After much insistence from Coach Jones, I let Rick take me back to the townhouse—leaving my car at the hospital—for a shower and a little bit of sleep. With the promise of Rick picking me up first thing in the morning, I don't think twice before I collapse face down on my bed. The soft cloud of pillows surrounds me as I will my mind to shut down and allow myself to sleep.

The next morning I'm pacing the sidewalk waiting for Rick's car. My body aches from the hours of sitting in the hard waiting room chair. Sleep didn't come easy. I was mentally and physically exhausted, but my brain would not turn off. I woke up this morning thinking it was all just a dream. That yesterday never happened. That there would be a good morning text waiting for me.

But it wasn't a dream, and reality is here, staring me in the face as I wait for Gregg's best friend to pick me up.

Glancing at my phone, I watch as the minutes continue to tick. Rick was supposed to pick me up at seven, and it's now approaching 7:15. As I'm about to call, I spot his blue Civic pulling into the parking lot.

"Sorry!" he blurts out as I open the passenger door. "The line at the coffee shop was ridiculous. I grabbed you a vanilla latte; I hope that's okay. I thought it was a safe choice." His energy is frantic, and the dark circles under his eyes tell me Rick wasn't fortunate enough to succumb to sleep.

My hand finds Rick's, which is perched on the gearshift. I can feel the stress radiating off of him. "It's perfect. Thank you."

Picking up the latte, I take a large gulp, welcoming the burn from the heat. Today is going to be a long day.

Fourteen hours later, I was right: it was a long day indeed.

And so was the next one.

Chapter 2

"**I**s that her?" My semi-sleeping mind hears whispers around me. I don't hear a response before the soft voice continues. "She's beautiful. Gregg wasn't lying."

Realization dawns on me that the dainty voice interrupting my sleep is Gregg's mom. She called me beautiful, which I'm far from. I can only imagine what I must look like after sitting in the waiting room for thirty-six hours. Coach and Rick have both tried to convince me to go home, but I refused. How could I go home when Gregg has told everyone I'm his girlfriend? The only reason I went home the first night was to pack a few essentials. There was no way I was leaving the hospital until we got answers, or I could see Gregg.

"She's pretty special," Rick replies, voice tinged with awe. "She's refused to leave."

Before Gregg's mom has a chance to respond, another voice fills the space. "You must be Gregg's parents."

"Yes, we are George and Gemma Carlton," Gregg's dad responds. "We are sorry we couldn't get here sooner. There was a storm moving through the Caribbean, and we couldn't catch a flight out sooner."

Sitting up, I adjust my sweatshirt, trying to put myself together before turning my attention to the doctor, but not before I catch Gregg's mom's eyes. A soft smile lines her face as her eyes glint under the fluorescent lights.

"It's nice to meet you. We finally have some answers and can allow Gregg visitors at this time. Would you like to discuss them in my office? I can take you to see Gregg afterward."

"That'd be great," George replies, placing his hand on the small of his wife's back as he gestures to Gemma to follow the doctor. She takes a few steps before turning around. "Come, Macy," she says, sweetness lacing her voice.

"Oh no, you guys can go ahead. I'll wait here."

"Nonsense. You're family," Gemma responds. Warmth spreads through me as I stand up and follow everyone through the doors.

We make our way to the doctor's office, and he tells us to sit. Taking a long breath, I do as I'm told, the all-too-familiar feeling of anxiety rushing back in like a tidal wave.

"The good news is we determined what caused the massive stroke. It took a lot of tests—some quite difficult—but after we conducted a TEE test—"

"I'm sorry, but what is that?" Gemma interrupts the doctor, and I fight the urge to smile, appreciating that Gregg's mom is as impatient as I am.

"A TEE test is a transesophageal echocardiogram test. It's rather difficult, but it's where we place a tube down his throat to look at his heart. While we were inside, we determined that Gregg had a PFO." The doctor pauses when Gemma's eyebrow quirks in confusion.

"Which is a patent foramen ovale. It means he had a hole in his heart that never closed when he was born. Most individuals would never know about this, and it is quite common. Gregg's neurologist and I have fought vehemently on whether he should have the hole closed with heart surgery. I believe now is the best time as he is already in the hospital and insurance will cover the surgery. However, the neurologist believes it could be too high risk in that it could trigger another stroke. I believe we should operate so Gregg never has to experience any of the issues and tests again. While the neurologist and I have fought to make the best decision for Gregg, we feel that it is up to him to decide on how to proceed."

Gemma clutches George's hand as shock spreads across her face. I'm having a hard time keeping up with all the medical information. I can't imagine how shocking this must be for his parents.

"Could this be why he gets migraines so often?" The question comes out of my mouth faster than I realize it. Heads snap in my direction, and I realize I spoke the question out loud instead of keeping it in my head.

"Absolutely. How often would he get migraines?" The doctor points the question at me as the Carltons face me.

"Weekly, for sure. Sometimes a couple times a week."

"That makes sense." Dr. Grey nods, chewing over the information. "Once we close the hole in his heart, his migraines should disappear or become very occasional."

"I think he should have the surgery," George states.

"Very well. We will confirm with Gregg before continuing, but if he decides to have the surgery, he can have it tomorrow."

"That soon?" Gemma asks, concern evident in her voice.

I reach over and wrap my hand in hers. It's a bold move considering we just met, but the moment felt right.

"Yes, we need to make quick decisions to get the situation resolved. Each minute that passes is critical."

Gemma lets out a deep exhale, and I notice the moisture sliding down her cheeks.

"Here," I say, handing her a tissue from the doctor's desk.

"If there aren't any more questions, I'll take you all to see Gregg now."

The walk to Gregg's room is quick; everyone is in a hurry to see him. Entering the room, the sight before us is a shock. Tubes, wires, and monitors are attached everywhere. Gregg looks so small and weak lying in that hospital bed with only a plain gown draped on his body. His tan coloring is gone, replaced with a pale purple tint. His blonde floppy hair is a mess. It stands on end and looks duller than I've ever seen. Gregg exudes sunshine, but lying there, he looks like a dark ocean that's anticipating a hurricane. The funny, outgoing, slightly nerdy guy that I've grown to know looks defeated. I feel my heart shatter at the realization we could've lost him.

"Hi, sweetie," his mom greets, making her way to his bedside.

"Mom," Gregg responds, throat scratchy from what I assume to be from the TEE test the doctor told us about.

Gripping Gregg's hand, his dad says, "Dad's here too."

"And your girlfriend. Gregg, you said Macy was special, but you didn't tell us how special. She's barely left the hospital since they admitted you," Gemma adds.

Gregg glances over his mom's shoulder as a sheepish grin takes over his face. I answer with a raised brow before making my way toward him.

"Hey, you." I reach past his mom, who is sitting on his bed, to squeeze his arm.

"Hey, Mace," Gregg responds, his eyes finding mine.

"I'm going to let you talk with your parents. I've got to run to the restroom, but I'll be back in a bit." Giving everyone a small smile, I quickly stride out of the room.

As soon as my feet cross the threshold and I'm in the safety of the hall, my body sags against the cold tile wall as sobs erupt from my chest. Placing my hands on my knees, I let the tears flow. It's at this moment I realize Gregg and I have been fighting feelings that have been there all along. From the moment we locked eyes at that party before the football game, we both knew we were supposed to be in each other's lives. We've both just been too stubborn to see it. But seeing him lying in that bed, so weak and vulnerable, was the wake-up call I needed.

I could've lost him.

I never told him this meant more to me than something casual, or that seeing his face is the best part of my day.

The surgery to fix his heart went off without a hitch. It was a long, stressful wait, but when the doctor came out and told us everything went well, you could feel the tension leave the room.

Thank God.

We wanted to see Gregg immediately, but the doctor told us we had to wait a while. Apparently, post-surgery recovery is just as important as the actual surgery. Part of the recovery is for Gregg to lie completely flat on his back for several hours.

Thinking of Gregg lying on his back brings me back to our second night together.

The two of us had run into each other at a pre-football game party fresh off our first night together. After the football game, the two of us went back to the Football House to party. At the end of the night, neither one of us wanted to call it, so we grabbed a ride share and took it back to my townhouse.

The next morning, I woke to the sound of rain, an uncommon sound as Texas was in the height of dry weather. Gregg was stretched out beside me, one arm tucked above his head, the other curled over his bare chest. My sheet was draped across his naked waist. All I could imagine at that moment was waking up to that sight every morning. To see his shaggy blonde hair wild from sleep and sex the night before. His naked, lean, athletic body stretched out, completely sated, waiting for me to curl up next to him.

But that day would never come because I told myself I was swearing off relationships all thanks to my asshole ex, who decided monogamy meant nothing to him as he slept his way through an entire sorority house and made me the laughingstock around campus.

"Thank you, Macy," Gemma says from beside me, interrupting my thoughts about her naked son.

Good grief, this is not the place to be doing that.

Glancing over, my face must show the confusion because she adds, "For being there for our son. It's been hard not having him down the road from us, but I'm so glad he has you here for him."

"You're welcome, Mrs. Carlton. Gregg's a wonderful guy. You and Mr. Carlton have done a great job raising him."

"Thanks, sweetie, but please call us George and Gemma. My in-laws are Mr. and Mrs. Carlton," Gemma says with a wink. I smile back at her. Gemma looks so young and put together. She looks like she could pass as his older sister, not the mom of a twenty-one-year-old son. I need to know what she uses for her skincare routine.

A few minutes later, the doctor comes back and escorts us down the hall to Gregg's room.

"We are very pleased with the results of the surgery. However, it appears that Gregg is still experiencing some aphasia, vision issues, and memory loss. These are all things that will eventually come back but will take time. There also seem to be some issues with the left side of his body. The strength in his left arm and left leg is quite weak. Again, all of this is normal, and with some physical and occupational therapy, we have no doubt Gregg will regain full strength. In the meantime, we are going to prescribe him some medication to help with pain and anxiety. I would also recommend that Gregg not live on his own."

"I thought you said everything went well?" Gemma asks. That same tinge of concern creeps back into her perfectly calm exterior.

"This is a preventative step until he regains full movement in the left side of his body. If he were to overdo it, he might lose strength, causing him to collapse. We don't know if he'll experience any more bouts of aphasia. I think it's best to have someone with him to help until he's strong and to notify us immediately if Gregg suffers from any sort of head pain."

Dr. Grey gives us a moment to let the words digest amongst the three of us. He continues, "Once you have a game plan for Gregg's care, we can discharge him tomorrow."

And with those parting words, the doctor leaves the three of us alone. The three of us walk into Gregg's room, the only sound our shoes against the linoleum and the faint whir of machines. I'm desperate to see Gregg again.

"I don't think I can take the time off of work to move this way," Gemma admits quietly.

"I can't either," George agrees in a hushed tone. "He's going to have to move home. It's the only solution."

"Solution for what?" Gregg asks sleepily, his parents' hushed tones clearly loud enough for him to hear.

Gemma takes a deep breath and glances at her husband again before answering her son. "The doctors won't release you unless you have someone to help you at home."

Gregg purses his lips, frustration lining his features.

I watch the conversation unfold, nibbling on my lower lip as I see everyone struggle to find the right answers for Gregg's dilemma.

And that's when it hits me.

The idea forms on the tip of my tongue before I even have time to think it through, and without hesitation, I blurt, "I'll stay with Gregg!"

Three sets of eyes find mine, and I want to sheepishly duck away.

"Mace—" Gregg starts, but I quickly cut him off.

"I'll move in," I reassure them with a smile on my face. Knowing that Gregg has a two-bedroom apartment, I can easily have my own space and won't be infringing on his recovery. I remember him saying that his parents found an off-campus apartment for him so that it's not as loud as most apartments on campus since he struggles with migraines—which we now know why—and the second bedroom is available for when they come visit.

My feet make their way over to Gregg, who is still lying flat on his back. Leaning down, I place a small kiss on his temple. Standing up, I smile at him, nodding my head. "Let me be there for you," I whisper, hoping only Gregg can hear me. His eyes soften, and I know at that moment he is going to agree.

"Are you sure? We can find other arrangements. Maybe look into a home nurse," Gemma says, interrupting the electric charge in the air.

"Of course I'm sure. That's what *girlfriends* are for."

Chapter 3

A few weeks ago, life said, "Watch this," and then scrambled our plans for what we thought our junior year of college would be.

No one would have guessed that Gregg, a healthy and athletic guy, would suffer a massive stroke at the age of twenty-one.

We couldn't have anticipated that with the stroke, he would be facing major heart surgery.

And I would have never predicted I would be moving out of the townhouse I shared with my two best friends to move in with a guy that I had slept with a few times, especially after swearing off relationships for this school year.

But here we are. Life has a cruel way of throwing a wrench in your plans whenever things are going well. I mean, it's 2022; nothing should surprise us anymore.

Since that day on the golf course, Gregg hasn't had any headaches. It seems repairing the hole in his heart really did fix his chronic migraines. Through both physical and occupational therapy, we are getting glimpses of the old Gregg again. The Gregg who always wears a smile, who says nerdy things—like talking like Yoda—and whose body hasn't betrayed him. Every day, I watch Gregg work hard to strengthen his muscles and regain the strength he once had. The first few weeks post-hospital were a battle. Depression and anxiety really sunk their claws into him. We might have been living under the same roof, but we were far from each other.

Since the two of us were in limbo about *what we were*, I opted to move into the guest bedroom. Gregg needed to work on accepting his new way of life—as temporary as it may be—and I didn't want to force my presence on him. I already felt like I had weaseled my way into his life. But when his parents said they were unable to move in with him and that his only option was to leave school, I couldn't let that happen. He was already so broken and defeated that I couldn't stand the thought of causing another life change for him. Gregg couldn't leave his friends, his classes—he'd fall behind— and he'd lose the independence he's created over the last two years at Central Texas University. Volunteering to move in was the only option I could see that didn't disrupt his life even more.

And selfishly, I wanted him close. I wanted to explore the feelings that being in that hospital made me face. I couldn't risk him leaving and letting whatever we had slip through the cracks.

The words "I'll do it" had never come out of my mouth so fast.

We were never supposed to be more than casual. But the stroke changed everything.

He needed me.

I wanted him.

And my heart couldn't say no.

Moving in together has gone relatively smoothly. We've settled into a sense of comfort between the two of us. Our once flirty relationship has settled into almost a friendship-only relationship. The two of us haven't had sex since the stroke, and I'm not sure if it's from the recovery or if things between us are just meant to be strictly platonic. Both Gregg and I are touchy-feely people and find ourselves constantly touching the other—a kiss on the temple, holding hands, pulling each other in for hugs—but nothing more than that. Would Gregg kiss all of his girl friends? No, probably not. But nothing has escalated to more than just friendly caresses. My mind is in a constant state of wanting to define the relationship, but I'm too afraid to push the subject. I can't imagine how awkward things will be between us if there's no hope for us to move into a relationship rather than this roommate/friendship relationship. For now, I'm living in a state of ignorant bliss.

Today is the first time we've been separated by miles, not from our schedules. Gregg's parents convinced me to catch a flight and head home for Thanksgiving break while they went to CTU and picked up Gregg. It's nice to get out of the apartment and give us a little distance, but the sad reality is I really miss him.

"Macy, would you like whipped cream on your pumpkin pie?" my mom asks from the kitchen. It's late, and my brothers have all gone home from our Thanksgiving lunch. It's just my parents and me at the house I grew up in.

Glancing up from the football game I'm watching with my dad, I look over the couch to find my mom. "Yes, please."

You have to have pumpkin pie with a little bit of whipped cream. It goes together like peanut butter and jelly, like cookies and milk, like Princess Leia and Han Solo. *Oh gosh, Gregg is really rubbing off on me.*

Mom brings in a tray with three plates of pumpkin pie and passes them out to us. She's forever in hostess mode. Always making sure that everyone is taken care of and always using different dinnerware she's picked up over the years.

Sitting down in the rocking chair across from me, Mom waits until I bring a bite to my mouth. Pumpkin pie is the far superior pie, and my mom's is always the best. The creamy pumpkin goodness melts against my tongue, and I let out a moan while my shoulders relax.

"The pie is so good, Mom."

She just smiles in return before turning her attention back to her own plate.

"How's things with Gregg?" my dad asks, his eyes never leaving the TV.

Quickly chewing, my head nods up and down. "They're good. His therapy seems to really be helping him."

"That's good."

A grating vibration comes from the coffee table, and my parents' attention whips to me while I lean forward and see Gregg's face lighting up the screen.

"It's Gregg; I need to take this."

Standing from the couch, I pick up the phone, swiping the accept button. My stomach is weighed down with a lead ball as uneasiness takes over. Gregg's emerald green eyes meet mine at the same time my dad is screaming about some *bullshit call*. I give him a look of annoyance as I carry my plate into the kitchen.

"Gregg, is everything okay?" I ask, panic lacing my voice.

He chuckles, his wide, bright smile spreading across his face. "Yes, Macy. Seriously, aren't you supposed to be enjoying time with your family?"

"I am. I just panicked when I saw your name flash on the screen." My chest relaxes as the worry slips from my body. Turning, I make my way over to the stairs before climbing them to my childhood bedroom.

"Nah, everything is fine. My parents just left already." That smile he was wearing starts to slip with frustration.

"Another case?" Gregg's parents are good parents. They care about the well-being of their son, but both of them live very hectic lives with their careers, which often have them leaving everything at the drop of a hat. His mom is the most requested paralegal at a highly sought law firm in Dallas, where his dad happens to be a named partner.

"Isn't it always?" He sighs, running his fingers through his shaggy blonde hair. "I don't even know why I bother coming home. The holidays suck."

An exasperated sigh leaves my lips. "They don't suck."

"Macy," Gregg interrupts. "They do. I know you have a book full of holiday memories that would rival a fairy tale, but not everyone has that. I hate the holidays. I hate the hoopla, the hype, and the disappointment. Thanksgiving is just another Thursday to eat supper alone. And Christmas is just another day where hopes are watched away by the ringing of a phone. I'm twenty-one. I've accepted it and don't care about the holidays. Not to mention their only son could've died, and they're too selfish to spend one whole day with me. I could've died."

I watch as a cocktail of emotions spreads through his features. Anger. Sadness. Realization. It's heartbreaking.

Empathy courses through my bones. It angers me so much that this amazing guy has been constantly disappointed by his parents, over and over. Never once did he get to experience the magic of Christmas, of Thanksgiving spent around a huge table with all of your relatives. And this year, of all years, they couldn't bother to spend time with him.

"I was so scared in that hospital room. I was terrified I wouldn't walk out of there. That one minor mistake would have me leaving this world early."

I watch as moisture gathers in his eyes before falling down his cheeks. He's showing a very real, very vulnerable side that he's kept inside for so long. This is the first time he's acknowledged how scared he was, how his life could've been cut short, and how he might not have had another holiday. My heart is breaking. I would give anything to wrap my arms around him right now.

Emotion clogs my throat. "But you're here, Gregg. You survived."

"Yeah, and where are they?" he shouts in frustration.

I quickly thumb the volume down, not needing my family to hear his vulnerability.

"I'm sorry, Gregg. I really am. I wish I could make things better for you. I wish I could take the pain away, I wish—" I stop as a lightbulb goes off in my head.

"What's that look for?" Gregg asks, curiosity getting the best of him.

"Give me one holiday season to change your mind about Christmas!" I practically scream through the phone; my mind spins with all the ways I could give Gregg the holiday experience he never had.

"No."

He flat-out refused. But I wasn't giving up. I, Macy Marie Miller, the lover of all things Christmas, was not about to live with a man who hates Christmas, all because he's never seen the hype.

"Please," I draw out, giving him the best puppy dog eyes I could muster.

There's a long pause on Gregg's end of the line. He scrubs his hand over his face, clearly trying to figure out the best way to respond. I watch as his features go from hard to something else. He's unhappy with me but also willing to compromise—one of my favorite things about him. "Fine, but I make no promises I'm going to enjoy it."

"Oh, I promise you'll enjoy it," I respond in a much flirtier tone than I intended. But I couldn't help but notice the heat flare in his gaze.

This is going to be a December he will remember.

It's been a week since Thanksgiving, and we are officially kicking off the Miller-Carlton holiday season tonight. When Gregg finally agreed to let me give him one chance to experience the true magic of the Christmas season, I knew I couldn't let him down. My type-A, Pinterest planning heart went a little crazy and began pinning all the ideas to make this the most magical holiday ever.

Glancing up at the clock, I will the hands to move faster. It's a quarter til five, and Gregg will be home from therapy in fifteen minutes. In today's session, he is working with one of CTU's trainers to get an update on his progression. The golf team needs biweekly evaluations to keep his scholarship records up to date.

I've spent all day—opting to skip class—turning our apartment into a winter wonderland. This is one activity I have been dying to do, and I hope Gregg loves it, or at least appreciates the change. Pine garland hangs from the mantle with fresh, dehydrated orange slices strung from end to end. Two cream-colored stockings hang underneath the garland. Battery-operated candles rest in their candlestick holders and are scattered across the mantle. A small fire is burning in the electric fireplace.

A six-foot artificial Christmas tree stands undecorated in the corner of our living room. It took me forever to haul the pieces out of my room and assemble the tree, but I thought Gregg and I could decorate it together. New, fluffy pillows and throw blankets sit on our couch. The whole living room feels warm and cozy—perfect for those rare, chilly Texas evenings.

String lights and garland hang from the kitchen window and the entryways, giving the apartment a soft, relaxing glow. I even swapped my usual bedding for a Christmas duvet and plaid sheets. Our apartment looks like the cover of a home magazine, and I'm quite pleased with the turnout, given I only had five hours to transform our very plain apartment into a winter wonderland.

Plopping onto the couch, my body eases into the cushions. I can already feel my muscles ache. A second later, my phone vibrates in my pocket, and I pull it out to check my notifications. There's a text waiting from Brynn—my best friend and former roommate.

The two of us have not been in a good place—it's my fault completely—but whenever I see her name light up my screen, my heart stops. Anxiety creeps in because I don't have any idea how the conversation is going to go. Since I blew up our living situation, Brynn and I have barely spoken. We've sent the occasional text message back and forth, but it's so obvious our friendship is severely strained.

This seems to be the story of my life with all of my relationships—including my friendship or whatever the hell Gregg and I are.

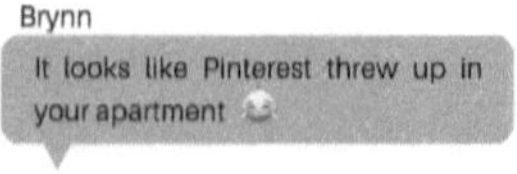

Closing out of the messages app, I open my camera and snap a few pictures, sending them as a way of response.

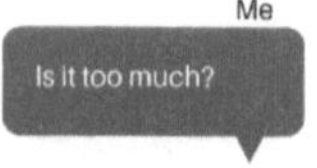

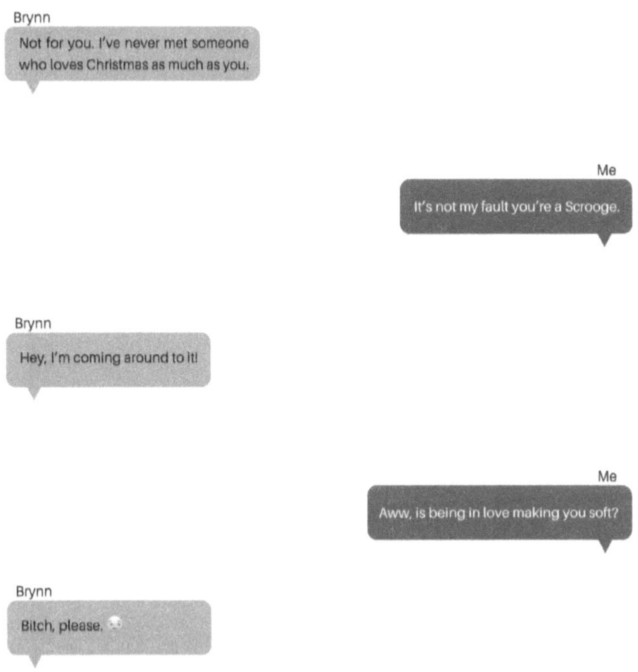

This year, Brynn finally woke up and realized she had feelings for her closest guy friend, Quinton. The two have always been inseparable and were killing us all with their denial of their feelings for each other. But when Brynn finally explained to us why she struggled to admit her feelings, we all understood her better. Now the two are blissfully in love, and I couldn't be more excited for her.

I just love love, even though love hasn't been kind to me. All I want is the kind of love that my parents have. The kind of love I watched Brynn and Quinton fight for. But like my mom always says, I have to kiss a few toads until I find Mister Right. I'm just hoping I won't have to kiss any more toads.

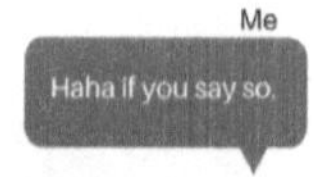

After hitting send, I hear a soft jingle of keys outside our door.

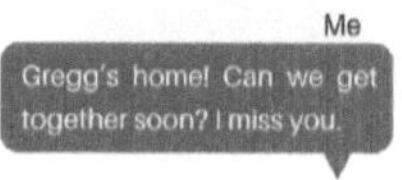

Rolling my eyes, I toss my phone aside. Standing up, I take one last glance around the apartment just as Gregg swings the door open. I watch as he pauses at the doorway; his eyes bounce from the corner of the living room where the tree stands toward the mantle that's fully decorated to me. I can only imagine what my face looks like. Perhaps a mixture of overly excited and worried—what I can only imagine a constipated elf looking like—because my stomach is in knots that he's going to hate the place.

His eyes finally land on me. He doesn't speak, just continues to stare at me with a blank expression. After what feels like an eternity, he slowly stalks toward me. There's a small limp to his step that you would never tell was there if you didn't know him before the stroke. He stops once his toes touch mine, his body hovering over my motionless form.

I can't breathe.

My chest feels like it could explode.

"Did you do all of this?" Gregg asks, his eyes boring into me.

"I-I-I did." I stammer out a response before meeting his gaze. I still can't get a read on how he feels. "Oh gosh, it's too much." The words rush. Tipping my head down, I feel my shoulders sag as a wave of embarrassment hits me.

Gregg's right hand cups my face as he tilts my head up to meet his eyes. Before I have a chance to react, his lips find mine. It's not a soft kiss but a hard, passionate one. A small gasp escapes, and Gregg uses the opportunity to plunge his tongue into my mouth. He's lapping, tasting, devouring me. I hear a small moan, and I don't know which one of us made the noise.

It's been weeks since we were intimate. Since his incident, we've been roommates who sleep in separate rooms and share small kisses and soft caresses. It's been so long since we've had sex that I've resorted to taking matters into my own hands.

He pulls back, both of us breathing heavily. "Thank you," he says, his voice barely audible. "Thank you for doing this for me—for us."

My shoulders ease, the tension I was holding in escaping.

"You're welcome. You wanted a magical Christmas." I shrug, gesturing around the room. "I hope it's magical enough."

Gregg leans back down and presses a chaste kiss on my lips. "It's perfect."

"I left the tree undecorated. I thought we could do that together."

"For sure. But I need to know what smells so good."

I laugh as he sniffs the air like a dog.

"Fresh orange garland," I answer, pointing to the mantle.

"You made that?" he asks, walking toward the mantle and rolling the garland between his thumb and pointer finger.

A smile spreads across my face. "I did. I started on them as soon as you left today."

"You're incredible, Mace. Seriously, I don't know what I would do without you."

At that, my insides feel all warm and fuzzy. His words make me want to melt into a puddle. We were never supposed to be more than one night, but after two, then three, one-night stands, it was clear we were drawn to each other. And now, after weeks of acting like roommates, I can sense that same magnetic pull begging us for *just one more night.*

Moving away from the mantle, Gregg makes his way over to the oversized couch and collapses in exhaustion. Therapy days always take a lot out of him. With his right hand, he pats the spot next to him. I take the hint and sidle up without another word.

Wrapping his arm around me, he pulls me closer and plants a kiss on my temple. "Do you think we can decorate the tree tomorrow? I'm not sure I have enough energy tonight."

"Of course we can. I thought we could order Chinese and watch a movie."

"You order the food, and I'll pick out the movie."

I snuggle in closer beside him. "Deal."

As Clark Griswold fills the screen and Chinese food fills our stomachs, I can't contain the smile that spreads across my face.

This just might be the most magical Christmas yet.

"Did you seriously buy me a hospital-themed ornament?" Gregg asks, staring at the red glass ornament with a white plus sign in the center wrapped in tissue paper.

Sheepishly, I watch his reaction as I try to figure out if he's upset with the ornament. "Yes," I answer, my voice shaking as I bite the inside of my lip to keep from letting my emotions get the best of me. "I always like to buy ornaments that represent the year, and I thought what better way to remember our first Christmas than with a hospital ornament."

Gregg turns his stare at me before he erupts in laughter. "Shit,

Mace," he says, holding his stomach from laughing so hard. "I can think of a million ornament ideas. Maybe a key for our apartment, or I don't know, a beer ornament for our drunken hookup. But this—this is epic."

"So you don't hate it?"

"Hate it? Are you kidding? I think it's great!" He stands up and walks over to the tree that we have just started to decorate. "It's going right in the center."

I breathe a sigh of relief. "Oh my gosh, you asshole! I thought you hated it. I was about to plunge myself off our balcony."

He hangs the ornament in the center of our tree, surrounded by red and silver glass ornaments. Still laughing, he turns and walks over to where I'm sitting on the floor. Bending down, he envelopes me in a hug and kisses me.

"I love it, babe. Seriously, I know that I'm a bit of a Scrooge, but I'm trying to be better. Christmas was always just Christmas at our house. My mom would try to make it special, but both she and my dad worked so much that we never formed our own traditions."

"I'm sorry."

He shrugs. "Don't be. My parents were good parents. I was just a surprise to two college students with big dreams. Neither one wanted to have kids, but they couldn't give me up either. It was always just my parents and me; we didn't have extended family. They did the best they could do given their careers. Our house wasn't a fairy tale. I knew they loved me in their own way, but it wasn't something we expressed. Honestly, the holidays were fine. I never went without gifts, but it didn't extend past that. There weren't days spent baking cookies or driving around to look at lights together as a family. I never knew more than just opening up gifts on Christmas morning, or whenever they were home to open them. It was just another day that had a few gifts to open."

Resting my head on his shoulder, we sit on the floor, staring at our tree. My heart hurts that his parents weren't able to give their son a more magical Christmas experience.

It's a good thing he has me this year.

Chapter 4

"Hi, Mom," I greet, answering her phone call.

Walking through the quad on campus, I weave through the chaos of students in search of an empty bench to sit at while I catch up with my mom. It's been a few days since we talked, which isn't like us, but life happens.

My mom and I have a really good relationship. I'm talking about the type of relationship where we are in constant contact with phone calls, texts, or sending each other videos on social media. She's always been my best friend, especially since I'm the youngest and only girl. My parents had four boys and somehow ended up with me eight years after my youngest brother. My brothers say I was an *oops*, but my mom says I'm the miracle baby that God knew they needed—especially after the boys.

"Hi, sweetie! How's your day going?"

"It's good. Gregg and I are both on campus for classes."

"Oh, that's right. I forgot today was Tuesday. Your dad and I have been so busy that I keep forgetting what day of the week it is."

"How's things at the Cozy Cabin?" Cozy Cabin is our business that has been in our family for three generations. It started as just two cabins and has since grown into twelve quaint cabins and a lodge that sits at the upper end of the lower peninsula in Michigan. Our cabins are nestled in the woods on a lake. It is the perfect destination for people wanting to get away and relax. During the cold months, the cabins are a great way to escape the holiday stress. You can relax in the hot tub while enjoying the winter wonderland. In the summer, it's the perfect destination to explore lake life. I loved visiting the property growing up.

"We are booked solid through the New Year," she answers with a sigh, and I can hear the exhaustion in her voice. "I'm so glad I told your father we should close for one week after the holiday season is over. I need a break."

"That's awesome that the business is doing great, though. Each year it gets more and more popular."

"Yes, it does. We have social media to thank for that," she says, referring to my sister-in-law, who took over the social media accounts last year. It was the perfect way for her to stay home with her kids while giving her a purpose outside of the house. Since she started doing reels and more behind-the-scenes content, the cabin is booked solid for weeks at a time.

"Speaking of the cabins," I start, "is our family cabin going to be vacant any time soon?"

"Yes, in two weeks. Why? Is my baby coming home?" Excitement laces her voice. My mom is always begging me to come home. She didn't understand why I chose a school so far away, but I needed to get out and see something outside of Michigan. Central Texas University just kind of happened. When I was applying for colleges, I picked ten random colleges, put them in a random name generator, and selected five schools to apply to. Talk about a crazy way to pick which colleges to apply to.

"Well, I was thinking about surprising Gregg with a trip to

Michigan. He's never seen snow, and I thought this would be a perfect way for us to do something he's never done before while still celebrating the magic of Christmas."

"Sweetheart, I knew I raised you well. I think that's a fantastic idea. I'll text you the dates, and we'll get everything planned. How is our sweet Gregg doing?"

A smile stretches across my face at the mention of Gregg. My parents haven't had a chance to meet him, and I wouldn't say they were thrilled I was moving in with a guy, but they've gotten to know him when I'm on FaceTime. I look around at the students hustling from class to class when my eyes find him from across the quad. "Speak of the devil, he's walking this way. But he's doing really well. The therapy is making a big impact on his movement."

"I'm so glad to hear that," my mother answers as I hear a bell chime from her end of the phone, signaling someone is at their front desk. "I've got to go, sweets. Give Gregg a hug from me, and I'll talk soon. Love you."

"Love you, too, Mom," I respond and hang up the phone just as Gregg approaches me.

Sitting down in the open spot next to me, Gregg's arm slides across my shoulder before he places a small kiss on my cheek. And damn, there goes that smile. This man. "How's your mom?"

I chuckle because, of course, he knew it was my mom on the phone. "She's good. They're super busy right now with the winter season in full force."

"I can imagine. You know, I never understood why people go on vacation in the winter to someplace cold."

"It's because you, my guy, are a Scrooge," I respond, poking him in the ribs where I know he has a ticklish spot. He shudders, slapping my hand away. "You've never experienced Michigan in the winter. Staying in a cabin is just so cozy. The exposed wood, the crackling fire, the hot tub surrounded by snow—it's just so enchanting. You feel like you're living in a storybook."

"I'll take your word for it, babe. So when's your next 'make Gregg love Christmas' activity?"

"Tonight. And you're going to love it!"

I had never been more grateful to have grown up with parents who love Christmas, especially when Gregg told me he wanted to really experience Christmas this year. Christmas is such a magical time of year, and I look forward to all of the holiday-themed events. It was super easy to plan out all of our dates. I just thought WWTMD—what would the Millers do?

Growing up, my parents would start decorating right after Halloween. In Michigan, it was quite often that the weather on Halloween was cold and nasty. On those days, we'd switch off the Halloween movies, flip on a Christmas one, and start decorating that night. The neighbors might've thought we were crazy, but we didn't care. We loved getting to sit under the glowing lights for a few extra weeks. And once Thanksgiving hit, my parents would start to spend more time at the Cozy Cabin, so the earlier, the better.

There's a knock at the door, disrupting me from my memories. Peering up from the full-length mirror, I spot Gregg leaning against my door frame. When I moved in, I decided I wanted to move into the guest bedroom. It just made the most sense at the time since Gregg was recovering—and battling self-consciousness with the way the left side of his body worked. I didn't want to be in the way. I figured we both needed a space of our own to escape when the days got too heavy.

His arms cross over his chest, making his muscles tighten, and I try not to undress him with my eyes.

"Ready?" he asks, taking in my outfit. Winter in Texas is still something I'm getting used to. It's definitely not like Michigan's blustering cold winters. Instead of chunky sweaters and thick socks, I'm dressed in a pair of ripped jeans, a lightweight camel-colored sweater, and heeled booties. I can still dress the part, just not as thick. The fashion major in me refuses to step out without looking chic and on-trend for the night.

Reaching behind me, I grab a matching camel, wide-brim wool hat off the bed. Placing it on my head, I take a final look at myself. With a quick fluff of my curled, light brown hair, I turn to Gregg. "Ready!"

Both of us start walking toward each other instantly. Meeting in the middle, he wraps his arms around me and pulls me into a tight embrace. "You look cute."

I chuckle at his compliment. "Thanks, handsome. Let's go."

Gregg leads me through the apartment and out of the front entry, only stopping briefly to lock the door behind us. I can't help but notice how much more motion he has in his left hand. Gregg Carlton will be back swinging a club on the green in no time.

Since tonight's adventure is a surprise, we walk through the chilled air to my silver Civic. Our destination is a quick drive from our apartment complex. Reaching over, I change the dials on the radio until the familiar jingle of Christmas music fills the air.

"You really are going all out with making me love Christmas, aren't you?" Gregg asks, glancing over at me.

"I have no idea what you're talking about. I happen to love Christmas music." Tapping my finger on the steering wheel, I belt out the lyrics to a popular song about giving your heart away last Christmas.

After a few minutes, I'm pulling us into the Festival of Lights.

It's a staple in the area with over two million lights. I love that you can drive through the space, and then at the end, there's a parking lot where you can get out, listen to live music, and view a few holiday displays.

"Mace, this place is insane," Gregg says in awe as he takes in the lighted signs that guide us into the park.

Opening the center console, I pull out a pair of glasses. "Here, I thought you might need them."

Glancing down, Gregg's eyes find mine. "You really did think of everything, didn't you?"

The doctor recommended that Gregg wear a special form of glasses whenever he's around bright lights or lights that flash. They help filter out the brightness so it's not such a sudden change that could trigger a migraine.

"Of course," I respond as Gregg grabs the glasses from my outstretched hand. His fingers linger on mine, and I feel that all-too-familiar electric shock sizzle on our skin.

Things have been weird between us since his stroke and the sudden roommate situation. Gregg has always been one to show how he feels, and the passionate kiss from earlier this week has me thinking there's more to us than just two people living together. But every time he shows me how much he craves me, he shuts down a minute later, leaving me to ponder what the hell just happened.

The two of us haven't discussed where we stand. Things aren't "official" between us. Well, Gregg has never asked to make things official. But what does that mean? Is it like high school, where you have to be asked to be boyfriend and girlfriend? Or, as you grow up, is it just assumed?

As much as I hate to be *that* girl, I need to know soon. I don't want to keep falling for him, only for Gregg to kick me to the curb when he's feeling stronger. While I need answers, a part of me isn't ready for a relationship. My last one really did a number on me, and I don't know if I can do that again.

But I can't get past seeing Gregg in that hospital bed.

I know I'm the one who set the boundaries. I'm the one who didn't want more between us. This year I was swearing off relationships, of falling in love, of being dependent on another person, but maybe I'm a liar. An overwhelming sense of desire poured over me when I was stuck waiting for answers from the doctors. Gregg is someone important to me. He's someone I can see myself building a relationship with. And I have to give us a shot. I have to see if he feels the same.

Shaking the thoughts from my head, I take a breath and focus on tonight's date. There's no sense in dwelling on the unknown right now. Driving forward, the two of us take in all of the light displays. There are lit-up Santas and reindeer. Flags of the United States and Texas line the drive. Thousands of strand lights arch above the driveway, welcoming you into the park.

"This place is like a Clark Griswold wet dream."

A cackle bursts from my lips at Gregg's very dirty take on the lights around us.

"Oh my God, only you would say something like that." Reaching up, I wipe the tears that are forming as I continue forward, driving with my knee.

Gregg's laughter fills the car. I love the sound of his laugh. It's hard to think I might not have heard it again if things had gone differently a few weeks ago. Not only with the stroke but also who knows what the two of us would've been.

I watch as lights flash across Gregg's face. I can't help but take in his sharp jaw that's covered in the smallest amount of blonde stubble. His dark green eyes warm with excitement as he takes in the display around us. My mind won't stop as I watch him. The two of us really need to have a conversation about where we are. I know that everyone thinks the two of us are dating, but at the end of the day, the only label I can put on us is *roommates*. I mean, things between us are good—really good—given the situation. But I'm a girl, and I need the definitive.

Following the last car out of the drive, I make our way over to the parking lot. Searching rows and rows, I finally spot an empty parking space between two SUVs. Putting the gear in park, I turn to Gregg and discover he's already watching me. Placing his arm on the center console before leaning over, his lips find mine, and he uses his right hand to grip the back of my neck, holding me to him. The kiss slowly turns heated as Gregg's tongue runs across the seam of my lips, begging for entry. Entry I easily grant him as I allow him to devour me.

Finally, with much reluctance, we pull away from each other.

"Thank you for taking me here," Gregg says, nearly breathless.

My chest heaves as I try to calm my racing heart and blood that is traveling to my core. It's been so long since Gregg and I have had sex, and each time he gives me a mind-blowing kiss, I'm like a dog in heat, just waiting for the moment to escalate.

It's not a matter of attractiveness that's preventing us; Gregg has been battling his mind. He's extremely self-conscious. He might not come out and say the words, but his lack of strength in his left side has messed with his head. I want so badly to tell him it doesn't bother me, but I don't want to draw attention to it. I don't want him to know I notice his hesitation to use his left hand.

Answering him with a smile, I turn to exit the car with the need for the chilly Texas air to cool me down. Gregg makes his way over to me and reaches down to take my hand in his. The two of us walk in silence as Christmas music fills the air.

As we near the entrance, Gregg pauses for a moment. Glancing up, I watch his eyes dart around before he's tugging me off to the side. It's then I notice the large photo booth. I can't help but smile, my cheeks blushing at the gesture. Reaching into his pocket, he hands the photographer some money and moves us in front of the backdrop. The photographer makes her way over to us and begins positioning us to pose for the shot.

"There, perfect," she says as she adjusts my hat. Rounding her tripod, the photographer makes a few adjustments to her camera. "Smile!" With a few clicks of her camera, her eyes brighten as she looks down on the screen. "These are perfect. If you could just leave me your phone number, you'll receive a text message with a link to your pictures."

Gregg gives the photographer his contact information while I look around us. Families are making their way into the park. Seeing parents armed with bags while pushing a stroller, I can't help but imagine myself in that role someday. I want to be the woman pushing a double stroller full of kids while my husband corrals the older ones. We'd be in coordinating outfits and spend the night taking selfies and making memories.

Gregg slides beside me, interrupting my daydream. Wrapping his arm around my shoulders, we make our way into the smaller Christmas displays. Sprinkled throughout the walkway are tiny Christmas villages set up on the ground. Looking down at them, you feel like you are looking at aerial views of actual small towns celebrating the season. It really makes me miss my small town in Michigan. But before I have a chance to dwell on it for too long, a sweet, nutty aroma takes over my senses.

"Oh my gosh," I gasp, pulling on Gregg's hand as I let my nose guide me, like a bloodhound on the trail. "We have to get some candied pecans. They're my favorite!"

Gregg laughs as I weave us through the crowd of parents wrestling their toddlers until I'm standing next to the metal trolly.

"Why, don't you two make a lovely couple," the older gentleman manning the trolly compliments.

Doing a double take, I can't help but stare at the portly man. He's dressed in a red fair isle print sweater. But what causes me to stare is his long white beard and wire-rimmed glasses that sit on his lower nose. He's the spitting image of jolly St. Nick himself.

"Thank you, sir," I respond, feeling the heat creep back into my cheeks. "Can we get two packages of your candied pecans and two hot chocolates, please?"

"Certainly," he says. "Would you like whipped cream on your hot chocolate?"

"Definitely," Gregg answers for the both of us, nudging my shoulder. His eyes find mine, and we both stare at each other. The green hues that line his irises look brighter against the glow of the lights.

Santa chuckles, and I swear the sound is like every TV Santa. Maybe I should ask him for one gift this season and see if it comes true.

After a few moments, we are off to the next Christmas Village, arms loaded down with delicious treats. Smiles stretch across our faces as soft moans escape my lips.

"I've got some nuts you can moan around," Gregg whispers in my ear, causing me to nearly choke on the pecans I'm chewing.

"Oh my God, Gregg!" I shout, slapping his stomach. I watch as a smirk forms on his lips.

"I'm sorry," he chuckles. "It was the perfect opportunity."

I just shake my head as the two of us continue our stroll. We see Christmas Villages displayed from all around the country—small towns to deserts to big cities. The attention to detail in each setting is remarkable. Curiosity getting the best of me, I can't keep my eyes from wandering to Gregg's. I watch the excitement light up on his face as he takes in each scene.

Looks like a few million Christmas lights and tasty treats are just what we needed. Slowly, I'm watching Mr. Scrooge's heart melt in the name of the Christmas Spirit.

Chapter 5

"**W**hat are we doing at the mall?" Gregg asks, disgust lining his tone. I laugh at his scrunched-up face.

"We're going shopping!" I exclaim, tossing my arms to the side and spinning in a wide circle. Watching me twirl does nothing to soften his expression. "Oh, come on. You have to buy Christmas presents."

"No, I buy gift cards. Gift cards are the best gift because then everyone can buy what they actually want, and we don't have to play the whole 'thanks for the gift, but I'm immediately returning it' game."

"Okay, Rachel Green, I don't know anyone who returns a gift as soon as they get it," I respond, rolling my eyes.

"Mace, everyone does it. Seriously, if it happens on 'Friends,' it happens in real life." With a shrug of his shoulders, Gregg starts walking toward a kiosk lined with gift cards.

"Don't even think about it, Carlton."

Stopping in his tracks, his head turns slowly over his shoulder, giving me a full view of his sharp, scruff-covered jawline. "Did you just last name me?"

I cross my arms over my chest, pushing my boobs up in the

process, and I watch his eyes flare. I quirk an eyebrow as I wait for him to stop staring at my chest. Slowly, his gaze finally meets mine, and a smirk twitches at the corner of my lips. "Alright, *Scrooge*. I'll make you a deal."

Turning completely around, Gregg makes his way back until he's standing toe-to-toe and peering down at me with a quirked brow. "What's your deal?"

"My deal is, you go *real* Christmas shopping with me and follow everything I have planned for our date in exchange for..." I pause, chewing on my bottom lip as I try to think of something that will get him to go along with this idea.

Turning his finger in the air, he interrupts the silence. "In exchange for..."

My mind can't think of what to bribe him with. My lady parts have a great idea that would lead to both of us naked and him on top of me, but I'm not sure if Gregg is ready. I don't take the bait, even though she's so lonely. "You get to play with my boobs?" I blurt out.

My eyes immediately squeeze shut as embarrassment spreads throughout me. I can feel my face flame and imagine it's as red as Santa's sleigh.

Gregg lets out a booming laugh that has people turning their heads in our direction. "That sounds like a win for you?"

"Let's just call it a win-win for both of us, and you get to experience the joy of Christmas shopping," I add.

With a roll of his eyes, he gestures for me to take the lead.

Walking hand and hand, the two of us make our way through the entrance. Squeaky shoes and voices bounce around us as Christmas carols play softly above. Everywhere I turn, store windows are decorated with winter scenery, and garland hangs from railings while twinkle lights glisten around us. Malls might be a dying thing, but I love the entire experience of visiting stores during the holiday season.

Christmas shopping was always a family affair growing up. The closest mall was forty-five minutes away from us, which meant shopping was a day-long ordeal. The seven of us would pack into the family Suburban and head to the city. Before we got to the mall, we'd always stop for lunch—usually a nicer restaurant that we don't visit often. Lunch was filled with laughter, jokes, and chaos, of course. I did grow up with four heathen brothers who loved nothing more than to cause mischief. My dad would try so hard not to laugh and partake in their antics while my mom would turn red from embarrassment. It's clear I inherited her embarrassment blush. As the youngest, I usually just sat back and watched, admiration in my eyes.

Shopping was always a treat, too. Those boys would constantly find themselves in mayhem in the mall. Mom and Dad would inherently have to separate us, otherwise, nothing would ever get done. Dad would take Max, the youngest boy; Miles, one of the twins; and me, while Mom would take the other two. Each group would shop for the other group, picking heartfelt gifts along the way. It wasn't always about getting what each other wanted or needed—it was about searching your soul and finding something special, something meaningful, that the other would appreciate far longer than the hype of whatever toy was popular.

Of course, we always wanted the latest and greatest, but I'll never forget the year my oldest brother scraped up some extra money to combine with the allowance our parents gave us to buy me a digital camera I had been wanting. I didn't even realize he knew that was something I wanted. When I asked him, he said he noticed that whenever we walked by them in the store, or when an ad would pop up, I would always pause with a knowing look on my face.

I cherished that camera.

"So how do I do this?" Gregg asks, interrupting my thoughts. We had managed to wander to the end of the mall, stopping in front of a department store that always looks beautiful with its neutral decor and lamps that lit up, cascading a warm, inviting glow.

"What do you mean?" I ask, gazing up at him.

"I mean, how do I shop for people? How do I know what they want without, like, a list or something?"

Reaching up, I place my hand over his heart. His breath stutters at the contact. I watch as his eyes darken, making his moss green irises look like a forest. "You search for it in here. What's something that would surprise your mom that you put extra thought into? What about your dad? What's a gift that would make them happy? It doesn't have to be a lavish gift. It could be something like a bath set for your mom—something that encourages her to find time to relax. Just something that comes from the heart."

With a deep exhale, I watch as his shoulders relax. "Come on," he says before walking into the department store.

Two hours later, with our arms bogged down, the two of us collapse on a bench outside of the food court. "I've never put so much thought into something in my entire life—not even golf." Gregg groans from beside me, making me laugh.

He's an insanely talented golfer. I've witnessed his concentration on the golf course. It's laughable that he says he's put more thought into shopping than golf. Resting my head on his shoulder, Gregg's hand finds my upper thigh, and the two of us sit, letting the calm pass over.

"I have one more thing for us to do."

At the sound of my voice, his deep inhale doesn't go unnoticed, and I know that Mr. Scrooge is starting to creep in.

"Let's get it over with," he says, nudging my head off his shoulder and standing up. We gather all of our bags before I lead us toward the food court. We pass family after family until we are standing in the line of Santa's Workshop.

"Hell no," Gregg states adamantly. A mom in front of us turns and gives Gregg that infamous *mom look*. I fight the giggle that wants to escape.

"Greeegg," I plead, peering up at him and batting my eyelashes.

His eyes snap shut, and his head turns to the ceiling before he replies. "Don't do that."

"Do what?" I ask, my voice turning softer as my hand runs up his chest.

Pushing my hand away, his eyes open, finding mine. "You know what," he grunts.

"Oh, come on. What better way to show that you are no longer Scrooge than by getting your picture with the big guy in red?"

"Ugh, I'm not fucking five," he growls, and the mom in front of us gasps at his language. He just rolls his eyes.

"Your mom would love it! Come on, Gemma would love a picture seeing you embracing the Christmas spirit." Gregg's eyes flash to mine in shock. "Oh yeah, I went there."

"You're cruel, Macy Marie. Just plain cruel." Reaching up on my tip-toes, I give him a very quick peck on the cheek. His arm wraps around my back, and he doesn't let me pull away when I try. Bending down, his lips find mine, planting a hard, closed-mouth kiss on my lips. Before pulling away, he whispers, "You're going to pay for this."

I shudder, his words causing flutters to go straight to the apex of my thighs as my imagination goes wild with sexual ways I could pay for my comment.

"Welcome to Santa's Workshop," the chipper blonde woman dressed as an elf greets us. She glances around, presumably looking for a child. Realizing there's no one else, she returns her attention to us.

"He needs to see Santa; he's been a *real* bad boy," I chime in before she has a chance to say anything.

"For fuck's sake," Gregg whines as the female elf gasps. I can't help the grin that takes over my face. The elf's mouth opens and closes like a floundering fish. Slipping my arm through Greg's, I usher us to the jolly man himself.

"I'm going to pay you back for that," Gregg hisses, and my body comes alive.

"Hi, Santa!" I greet. "This is Gregg, and he seems to have lost the Christmas spirit. Do you think you can help with that?"

A deep chuckle comes from the big guy. "Why yes, I can!" he replies in a deep, jolly voice. "Come, sit, Gregg."

With one last side eye from Gregg, he straightens his shoulders and slaps on a fake smile before taking a seat on the armrest of Santa's red velvet chair. I feel his eyes on my back as I walk back over to the blonde elf, who has since moved behind a digital camera.

While I watch the girl in the elf costume situate the camera, Gregg leans closer to Santa and speaks in a hushed tone I'm not able to hear, but whatever it is has Santa looking over at me. I watch as Santa's eyes soften, blanketing me in a feeling of uneasiness. Feeling my cheeks heat, I tear my gaze away from the two men, who, by the way, look absolutely ridiculous sitting together.

"Do you mind if I take a picture on my phone, too?" I ask the elf.

She gestures for me to go ahead. Sliding in front of her camera, I position the camera and take a couple of candid photos of Gregg and Santa. "Okay, you two." I direct my words to the men on the red chair. "Say, 'bowl full of jelly.'" Gregg and Santa turn their attention to me, and both smile widely. Quickly, I thumb out a few adjustments on the camera before snapping a few shots. With a smile and nod, I let the two know that I got the picture.

"Wait," Gregg shouts before I have a chance to move away.

"Come get a picture with us!"

Glancing at the blonde elf, she smiles, but her eyes reflect her annoyance. Hastily, I make my way over to the opposite side of Santa's chair. We quickly get into position, me leaning on the arm with my legs extended in front of me and Santa wrapping his arm around my waist in a purely platonic manner. Smiling at the camera, a bright flash comes from the equipment, momentarily blinding me. No wonder so many small children scream when they meet a holiday figure.

After paying for our prints, we watch the next family approach Santa while we wait for our images. Santa's helper brings us our envelope of pictures, and Gregg snatches them before I have a chance. He reaches down, grabbing our shopping bags, and I watch as he practically flies out of Santa's Workshop.

"Don't you dare destroy those pictures! We are putting it on the mantle." I shout after him. He turns his head and gives me a wink.

With that wink, I see Scrooge melt away.

And so do my panties.

Chapter 6

December is flying by. We spent the last few days with our noses in our textbooks as we prepared for finals. Now that they are over, CTU is officially on winter break. Not much has changed for us. We are still in a state of limbo, no matter how hard I try to figure out where we stand.

A week ago, Gregg was giving me a panty-melting wink, only for it to fizzle into nothing. We came home from shopping completely exhausted. I watched as he retreated into his room while I stood in the living room, wondering what the hell I did wrong.

Curled up on the couch, a cute Hallmark movie plays in the background while I sit with my sketchpad in my lap. This next semester, I'll have to create a clothing line, and I'm trying to get a jumpstart on the designs. The professor gives us the flexibility to design whatever we want—casual, evening wear, business attire, swim, menswear— and bring three designs to life for a campus-wide fashion show.

One lucky student will get the opportunity to work closely with an actual designer in New York City for six weeks in the summer. It would be the opportunity of a lifetime.

Too bad for me, I'm stuck with colored pencils scattered

around and only a few scribbles in my sketchpad to show my work. My mind is on overdrive. Whenever my brain is focused on all the things I need to do, my body shuts down. I find myself wasting time, staring off into space. In the past, I've always reached out to my best friend, Brynn. She always knows how to snap me out of my funks, but with our friendship being in a weird place, I feel weird about asking her for help.

Screw it.

Before I can react, I'm reaching for my phone. Clicking the all-too-familiar name, I wait for her to pick up. My chest feels heavy, and my lungs are struggling to fill. My mind is on a tailspin, and I've never felt so lost and confused in all my life. I just don't understand.

"Macy?"

"Brynn. Hey, hi, I um," I stutter, trying to get the words to come out of my mouth.

"Mace, is everything okay?" Brynn asks from the other end of the phone.

Great. On the verge of a mental breakdown, I picked up the phone and called Brynn.

I know our relationship is rocky, and I know we desperately need to have a conversation to fix things, but right now, I just need a friend. And I'm hoping the damage I caused hasn't been enough to ruin any type of relationship between us.

"Yeah, um, everything is," I start, inhaling a deep breath. "No, I just really need a friend. I know that I screwed up, and I left things on a terrible note between us. But I just don't want to be alone right now."

"I'll be right there," Brynn responds, not missing a beat.

My life seems to be in a constant state of confusion. I was really hoping Gregg and I's day of shopping would change things, but here's to hoping the close proximity and no distractions during the break will motivate a conversation. I know I could initiate the topic, but I'm just terrified to bring it up. I've caused so much drama with my friends that I'm terrified to add unnecessary drama with Gregg.

But with both Gregg and I staying at the apartment for the break and our friends staying on campus, too, I'm hoping there will be a chance for all of us to spend time together. I've never been so grateful for football in all of my life. The CTU football team is undefeated and preparing to play in the National Championship, which means everyone has to stay at CTU. Brynn is over the moon excited for Quinton and the boys, and the fact she doesn't have to be alone for the holidays.

It seems like forever ago when we were all partying before the opening game. A lot has changed since the beginning of the school year, and again, I can't help but blame myself for the tiff in our friendship. Brynn is in a relationship, which might be the biggest shock. I'm barely speaking to Chloe, who was—is—my best friend. And what I thought was going to be a year of self-discovery and staying single ended with me moving in with a boy. It looks like the girls are growing up—and growing apart. Which I both love and hate.

The three of us have been thicker than thieves since we met our freshman year. I hate to see how our friendship has changed. All of us are on opposite ends as we navigate and try to find solace in the world of college. Brynn is floating on a cloud with her and Quinton's relationship. Chloe is still living in a world of fiction instead of owning her feelings. And I'm stuck in a roommateship.

Chloe has been especially hard to decipher lately. She'd much rather keep her nose in a book and live in a reality of pretend romance than step outside her comfort zone and go after what she wants. Or who she wants. Anyone with eyes can tell she has a thing for Cody, our friend who is on the CTU baseball team. There's tension between the two of them that I'm not sure anyone else has noticed, but I have. It's what caused our biggest fight and our current friendship predicament.

"Yo, Earth to Macy," Brynn says, snapping me from my thoughts.

"Thanks for coming over," I say, swiping another coat of bright red nail polish on my fingers.

"Bitch, stop thanking me. It's what friends are for," she says, swatting my ponytail as she walks past me to the couch. I watch as she moves around, fluffing and folding pillows until they are at the perfect angle for her to relax into the cushion. "Is tonight the night you two finally get it on?"

I roll my eyes, bringing my hand up to blow on the wet lacquer. "I'm not holding my breath. Don't get me wrong, I totally understand why we haven't had sex yet. I mean, *he did* suffer a massive stroke. But his recovery is going great. The caresses and lingering glances, not to mention the heated kisses, have me constantly squeezing my legs together. Even if it's not sex, I just want an orgasm I don't give myself."

"Okay, first of all, no one is judging you for wanting to have sex with your boyfriend, roommate, whatever the hell you two are—which you need to figure out. You're in close proximity; you're going to have urges."

"Wait," I interrupt. "I never had urges when we were roommates."

"Speak for yourself," she responds, waggling her eyebrows. I toss the throw pillow that's sitting next to me at her face. "I'm kidding! Sorry, Mace, you might have the best vag around, but I like dick."

"Do you always have to speak what's on your mind?"

"Hey, I am who I am. Love me or hate me," she says, throwing her arms out to the side.

Brynn oozes confidence and sex appeal. She has a reputation on campus, and it's not from her bragging about her lifestyle. Girls around campus are catty with their jealousy, but instead of supporting her, like they should, they tear her down with their dirty looks, nasty words, and their own insecurities. It doesn't help that her beauty draws attention. She's stunning in a natural, effortless way, and guys notice, all wanting to warm her bed. But as soon as she worked out her past trauma, Quinton helped her see that she wasn't really living life—she was just surviving. Since then, she's turned all that sexuality towards Quinton. The two can't get enough of each other.

"We wouldn't change you, B. I love my Wilder."

"I love you too, babe." Leaning down, she places a kiss on my cheek.

The conversation comes to an end, and a comfortable silence fills the space. I hit play on the remote as one of our favorite Housewives shows fills the screen. Finals have us behind on our reality TV. After a few minutes, I hear Brynn rustle on the couch.

"I just don't get it," she starts, causing me to turn my attention toward her. "Why didn't you just tell us what was going on? We would've understood."

"Right, like you were so open with your past," I retort, referring to Brynn's traumatic past that she decided to keep secret for two years.

"Touché," Brynn adds, rolling her eyes.

"I think I was just in panic mode. I was freaking out and exhausted. I have never had to face anything like that before. My only priority at that moment was Gregg. The doctors wouldn't release him until there was proof of someone living with him. My brothers were pissed I was moving in with some guy. And my parents were concerned that I was taking on more than I needed to. I couldn't face the questions from you and Chloe."

The confession spills from my lips. I knew what I was doing was shitty. It wasn't like me to just up and abandon my friends, but I just couldn't face any more judgment. I had made my peace with the situation and was exhausted from hearing all of the concern and discouragement from the people I loved.

"Alright, so how are you *really* doing with everything? And don't bullshit me," she asks, turning her head until her gaze is searing the side of my face.

With a deep sigh, I think for a minute before answering. "Honestly, I'm fine. I really am, but Gregg and I need to have the 'what are we' conversation. I've been avoiding it."

"No shit," she says instantly. "But I'm not asking about that. I want to know about you. This has to be a lot for you to handle."

Pausing, I wrack my brain as I try to sort out the emotional rollercoaster I've been living. "It just put a lot of stuff into perspective. So much of life is spent running from one thing to another that it's hard to stop and live."

"I know all about that," she murmurs, and I give her a small, knowing smile. When Brynn was sixteen, she lost her twin brother and her boyfriend in a tragic car accident. She spent the last five years running on autopilot and acting out instead of working through her grief.

"I think that's why I'm scared to talk to Gregg. I want to keep living in this happy little bubble where everything is just perfect."

"But that's a fairy tale. What are you afraid of? We all know the man is head over heels in love with you. We've known it since the beginning of the school year, after what, your second *date*." Brynn says date using both her hands to make quotation marks.

"You're one to talk," I retort, referencing her being in denial about Q.

"Stop deflecting. We aren't talking about me."

"I know. And I love him, too. It's just…we haven't talked about our future together." My gaze falls to my lap, where I begin picking at fuzz that's not really on my pants.

"Macy, the guy called you his girlfriend to his parents. He obviously sees a future with you. And tonight, after he sees you in your sexy outfit, he'll be dropping to his knees, begging to be yours forever."

"You're right. I need to get out of my head," I say.

"I'm sorry, I didn't hear you over all the clapping in my head." Both of us laugh. My smile doesn't leave my face the whole time Brynn is here. She really is the absolute best friend a girl could have. She has a way of building your confidence without you realizing it. I just wish more people got to know the real her and not the tough persona she exhibits.

After our second episode of *The Housewives*, Brynn follows me into my room so I can get changed for my night out with Gregg. Tonight, the two of us are heading downtown to the makeshift ice rink. Gregg has never been ice skating before, and while that won't change tonight, I thought it would still be fun to go down and watch others skate.

"Okay, what do you think about this outfit?" I ask Brynn as I hold up a white, off-the-shoulder sweater and a black mini skirt while pulling out my black, thigh-high boots.

Her eyes practically bulge out of her head. "Okay, this look is hot. I knew you said you had a sexy outfit planned, but damn, girl!"

"So it's okay?" I ask, chewing on my lip as the insecurity washes over me.

She stares at me, eyes wide as if the answer is that simple. "Yes! Now hurry up and change! Oh, do you have black tights?"

Rummaging through my closet, I find a pair of thin black tights to layer under my skirt. Sliding out of my joggers, I work to pull the tights up my leg. If these didn't make my outfit sexier, there's no way in hell I'd be putting them on.

Once my tights are secure, I slip into my skirt, fastening the button as I take in my appearance. Tossing my oversized shirt off and into my hamper, I carefully place the sweater over my head, careful not to get any makeup on the neck.

Tilting my head back and forth, I appreciate the look.

"Here," Brynn says from behind me. She's holding a makeup brush and a highlighter palette.

Turning toward her, I watch as she dips the brush in the gold glow powder before brushing it across the swell of my breasts and the sharp angle of my collarbone. "There. You just needed a bit more glow to the goods."

She's right, I think as I face the mirror again, scrutinizing my reflection. With a few flicks of my wrist, I secure my hair in a top knot, pulling a few face-framing tendrils out, not wanting my hair to take away from my new glow and the outfit. Reaching for the can of hairspray, I let Brynn spritz the back of my hair as she wipes my stray hairs up towards the hair tie. She's just finishing the last spray as we hear footsteps down the hall. Before Gregg enters my room, Brynn winks at me through the mirror.

"Oh, sorry," Gregg starts, but he doesn't get any more words out as his eyes trail my body.

"Have fun tonight, you two," Brynn purrs. With a quick peck on my cheek, she's walking out the door, patting Gregg on the shoulder as she passes him.

"You look incredible," Gregg rasps before clearing his throat, his attention never wavering from me.

A blush creeps over my face as I watch his eyes smolder as he gives me his undivided attention.

"Thanks," I respond, zipping up my last boot.

"I-uh-I'm going to go change," Gregg blurts, shaking his head. With quick paces, he leaves my room and heads for his. I exhale a sigh of relief, a triumphant smile finding my face. It's good to know that I still affect him as much as he affects me, which was evident by a certain outline I saw growing in his *gray* sweatpants.

"So we aren't ice skating?" Gregg questions as he takes in all the people on the rink.

Shaking my head, I reach inside my bag and pull out an insulated tumbler. "I thought we could enjoy a cocktail while watching people fall?"

He laughs, taking the tumbler from me. Opening the lid, he brings the liquid to his lips. "Bourbon sours?"

I smile. "Only your favorite."

"Thanks," he says, taking another sip before handing the tumbler back to me. I take a small swig and turn my attention to the rink in front of us. "Do you know how to skate?"

"I do," I answer. "The pond at the cabins freezes for most of the winter. Mom and Dad started teaching us how to skate when we were young. When the boys got older, the four of them would play two on two hockey. I'd sit with my parents or skate off to the side while we watched the boys. I was too young at the time to play with them."

He nods as he listens to my story. "Maybe someday you'll be able to show them up. The feisty little sister kicking their asses."

I laugh, resting my head on his shoulder.

The two of us spend the next hour sipping our shared cocktail as we watch couples try to navigate their dates on skates.

"If it isn't Gregg Carlton," a voice says from the rink. We watch as a couple skates toward the edge where Gregg and I are leaning against the wall.

"Ricky!" Gregg yells toward his best friend. I watch as Rick's shoulders deflate at the nickname Gregg called him.

"Dude, what have I told you about calling me Ricky?" Rick's exasperated tone has me laughing. I haven't seen much of Rick since the hospital. Our time spent together will always mean a lot to me. I don't think I could've made it without his shoulder to lean on.

There's a petite brunette standing next to Rick. She's dressed in a black trench coat and leggings. A pom beanie sits on her head, her brown hair in two braids that hang over her shoulder. "This is Zoey," Rick introduces. "Zoey, this is Gregg and his lady friend, Macy."

"Hi," she greets, her voice soft and quiet. The three of us exchange pleasantries.

"How are you feeling, man?" Rick points the question to Gregg.

"Good," Gregg replies with a shake of his head.

A smile breaks across Rick's face. "Hell yeah, we'll have you back on the green in no time."

If I hadn't been watching Gregg closely, I would've missed the slight twitch of his smile, causing it to fall slightly. Gregg hates any talk of golf. He hates feeling like he's weak. "You know it. Tell the guys to get ready to have their asses kicked."

Rick nods. "A bunch of us are going to the new golf simulator on campus Friday. You should come if you are around."

"Yeah, man," Gregg answers.

After a few minutes of small talk, Rick and Zoey skate off, leaving Gregg and me standing on the side of the rink. Gregg tried to hide how the words affected him, but I watched as his demeanor changed.

Knowing our night is over, I nudge Gregg's shoulder and take one for the team. "Let's head home. I'm getting sleepy."

He nods, and the two of us walk the short distance to the parking lot.

One day at a time.

Chapter 7

"ARE YOU TWO JUST FUCK BUDDIES?"

My nerves kept me from sleeping. All night, I tossed and turned. And tossed and turned some more. I could not get my mind to turn off.

What if he hates it? What if I completely missed the mark, and it's too late to do anything about it?

Today's plan is the biggest surprise this month, and I'm hoping—and praying—Gregg loves it. I was so anxious for his reaction, I ended up texting Brynn at 2:45 this morning.

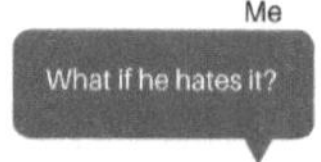

I laid the phone on my chest, staring at the ceiling. I didn't expect a response, but to my surprise, she said:

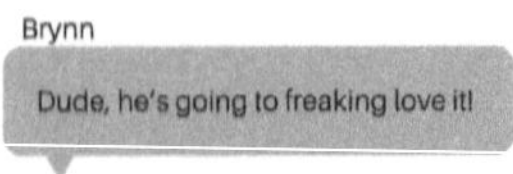

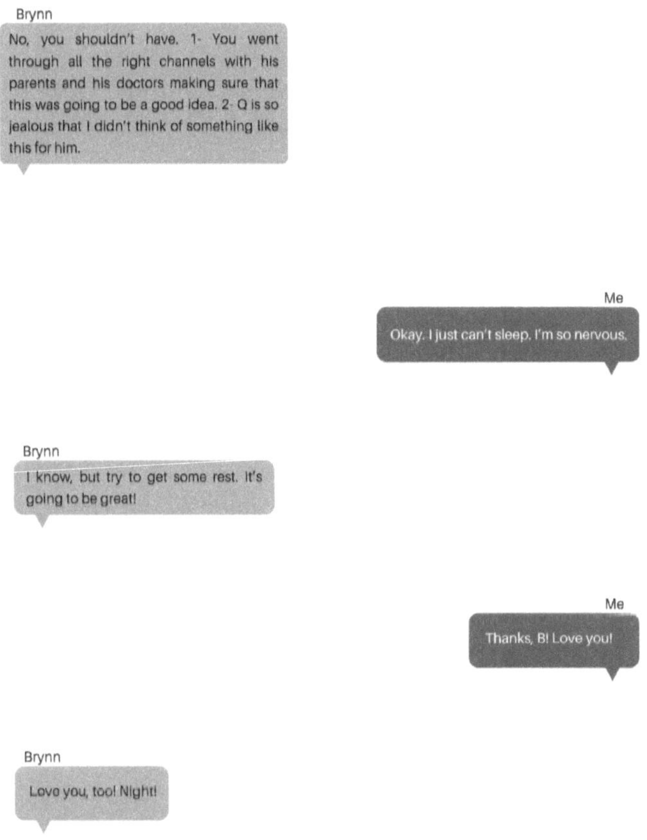

Our conversation was enough to help lull me back to sleep, but then my alarm blared, bright and early, at 5:15 a.m.

Now, I scrub the sleep from my eyes, tossing the covers as the cold air hits my exposed skin. Goosebumps break out as I fight with my mind not to curl back underneath the warm covers.

Get up! Get up! Get up!

With one last stretch, I make my way out to the hall bathroom. The apartment is peacefully calm. The hallway glows from the lit

Christmas lights, and there's not a noise around. This is why I love mornings. I love the calm and the quiet. I love the feeling of being the only one awake.

Flipping on the light switch, I wince as the bright light blinds me, blinking rapidly until my eyes adjust. Once I feel like I can see again, I quickly use the restroom and brush my teeth. There is no way I was waking Gregg with dragon breath, no matter how *in* dragons are right now. Game of Thrones has everyone wanting a dragon, while I just want Jon Snow.

Turning the knob to Gregg's bedroom door, I quietly make my way over to his king-sized bed. Soft snores fill the room as I try to find Gregg's sleeping form in his dark room. It doesn't help that he sleeps in complete darkness—black-out blinds and curtains, and his bedding is dark gray. His room is like walking into a cave. After a couple of seconds, my eyes adjust and make out Gregg's body. His back is curled away from the door. Slowly, I make my way over to the bed before pulling up the covers and slipping underneath them. A soft hum in appreciation escapes his lips as my chest meets his bare back. His arm finds the back of my leg as he pulls me closer to him. His warmth seeps into me, and I'll gladly debate that this sensation is better than the warmth of coffee spreading through your veins in the morning.

"Good morning," I whisper in his ear.

"What time is it?" he rasps, burying in his sheets. My arm wraps around his middle, and I lightly trace the line of his abs.

"It's early, but I have a surprise for you."

Turning around, Gregg nestles in my chest, peppering kisses down my neck. "What kind of surprise?"

"The kind where I need you to get out of bed and trust me." Gregg's head moves backward until his eyes find mine. With a lift of an eyebrow, he waits for me to elaborate. With a small smile and a quick peck on the lips, I move out of his grasp. "Come on. We need to leave in thirty minutes."

Half an hour later, the two of us are finishing our mugs of coffee in the kitchen. Rinsing out his cup, Gregg eyes me from where I sit at our breakfast table. I watch as his eyes bounce from me to the front door, confusion lining his face. "Why is my suitcase sitting at the front door?"

"We're going on a trip," I mumble from behind my coffee mug.

"I'm sorry, I didn't quite catch that," he responds, eyes narrowing. "Did you just say we are going on a trip?"

Standing from my seat, I walk until I'm standing in front of a very confused Gregg. "Remember when I woke you up and told you to trust me?" He nods. "Okay, well, I cleared it with your doctors, and I have a little trip planned for us."

"Macy—" he starts before I press a hand to his mouth, silencing him.

"Just trust me, okay?"

With a nod, I remove my hand from his mouth. The two of us make our way to the front door, grabbing our suitcases as we head out.

"Michigan?" he asks, staring at the boarding pass.

"Surprise?" I say with more of a question than excitement.

"Mace, why are we flying to Michigan?" Gregg asks, staring at the ticket and then back at me.

"We are flying to Michigan to stay at this super cute place called the Cozy Cabin where your wonderful girlfr-roomie-whatever she is to you planned an epic weekend away." I rush the words out, mushing the labels together because I still don't know what to define us as.

Thankfully, the announcer comes on, calling out our flight and saving me from the embarrassment. "Come on, or we will be late!"

Picking up my carry-on, I head toward the forming line. A few seconds later, Gregg joins me. The two of us follow the line of people onto the aircraft. Glancing at the passing numbers, we watch as they climb until our seats come into view in the middle of the plane. Gregg gestures for me to take the middle seat—lucky me—while he gets the aisle seat.

"So, how long have you been planning this trip?" Gregg asks as he scrolls through the in-flight entertainment options. I watch as he thumbs through the endless movies. There are a few Christmas ones sprinkled in the mix. Reaching over, I place my hand on his thigh. With a small squeeze, I gain his full attention.

Nervously, I pause before my admission spills from my lips. "I've been planning this trip for a couple of weeks. I was talking with my mom, and she mentioned that there was a cabin free this weekend. I asked her if I could use it to surprise you." I watch his eyes roll—Gregg still hates the attention on himself. "Mom thought it was one of my best ideas."

He chuckles. "*Of course* she did."

"What?" I ask in an exasperated voice. "She did."

His head finds the seat, and I watch him go from gazing at me to glancing at the screen in front of him. Before he has a chance to scroll through the movie options again, I reach over and tap *Christmas with the Kranks* on his screen, and I do the same on mine.

"Let's watch it together," I say. "On the count of three, ready?"

Gregg cocks an eyebrow but obliges. "Fine. One. Two."

"Three," we both say at the same time before pressing play.

"Can I take this blindfold off yet?" Gregg asks, annoyance lining his voice.

Our plane landed an hour ago, after two delayed flights and a nearly forty-minute drive to the property. Both of us are exhausted from all the stress. Flying is convenient, but I'll take a long road trip any day. Grateful doesn't even begin to describe how I felt when my dad texted that the property driver would be waiting to pick us up. One of the perks of staying at our venue is we have a staffed driver available to pick up and drop off guests at the airport since the closest one is forty to forty-five minutes away, depending on traffic.

Pulling into the property's driveway, my mouth drops in shock as I find a horse-drawn carriage waiting for us. The Cozy Cabin has six Clydesdales—three are the traditional bay colors with white markings, two are black with white markings, and the sixth is grey with white splatterings throughout his coat. When the property was first acquired, Clydesdales were used to help clear out the land from the trees and work the ground. Now having the horses is a tradition that we use to take the guests on tours around the property.

But standing before us, the six beautiful horses are harnessed to a garland-lined red wagon. It's a majestic sight, and I'm so glad I had the thought to blindfold Gregg on our drive. He might've objected to great lengths, but I know that seeing and feeling the snow for the first time, in this setting, is going to be worth it.

"Just a couple more minutes," I tell him. Adjusting myself in the seat, I reach to open the door.

"Please sit in the warm car while I transfer your bags over," our driver says.

I don't object as I glance at the car's thermometer. Twenty-nine degrees. *Houston, we aren't in Texas anymore.*

"I could've grabbed our bags," Gregg grumbles beside me. It's funny to watch his head turn from side to side as he tries to gather his surroundings.

I sigh. "Yes, I know. But I promise this will be all worth it. Do you trust me?"

Outstretching his hand, he waves it around the air until he finds my thigh. "We've been through this. I trust you completely."

"Okay then." I don't have a chance to add more to the conversation before our driver opens my door.

The cold air hits us both, and we can't help the shudder that slides down our spines. My mom told me she would take care of the winter gear for Gregg—my brothers had extras—which means Gregg isn't dressed for the Michigan winter.

I thank the driver before stepping around the back of the car towards Gregg's door. Before I get a chance to open his door, I'm hit in the chest with a snowball. Glancing down at the mashed snow, I slowly bring my gaze up, eyes narrowing. Standing in the snow at the bottom of the wagon is Miles, one of my older brothers.

"You did not just hit me with a snowball," I say in shock.

Looking me up and down, a grin spreads across his face. "Yep. It sure looks like I just did."

Shaking my head, I let the laugh fly out. As much as I want to run and jump on my older brother, I need to get Gregg out of the car before he loses his shit.

"Miles, do you have your phone?"

"Yes," he answers hesitantly.

"Can you take some pictures or videos for me?"

"Sure thing, Sis. Mom told us it's your guy's first time in the snow." Of course she did. "Who hasn't seen snow?" I hear him mumble.

Ignoring him, I open the door, reaching down and grabbing Gregg's hand. Guiding him out of the car, I hear the crunching of the icy snow mixture below our feet. I watch as a slow smile melts onto his face. If he's excited just from the sound, he's going to freak out once he takes it all in.

The scene in front of us looks like a set of a Hallmark movie. Dusk has fallen over the property as darkness starts to creep in. The horse-drawn carriage sits in eight inches of snow. Pine trees surround us. And in the distance, you can see the bright glow of Christmas lights twinkling as they hang from the wooden cabins. It's breathtaking.

I missed being home.

Reaching up on my tiptoes, I slide my hands around his neck. Pulling his mouth to mine, I plant a kiss against his lips. "Ready for this?" I whisper against his lips.

"I'm so ready," he answers. With those words, I slide the blindfold over his head and watch in amusement as Gregg blinks, his eyes focusing on the picture in front of him. "Holy shit."

A wide grin breaks out on his face, stretching from ear to ear, and I can't help the joyous expression that breaks free across my own face. Bending down, Gregg gathers a scoop of snow in his hands. He packs the white dust, rolling it around his palms before tossing it back down on the ground. In the next move, he's scooping me up in his arms. Our bodies are flush as one of his hands finds the back of my head, and then he's pulling me into him. Lips finding mine, I gasp at the force, granting him access to slip his tongue into my mouth. It's a searing kiss that has all the blood rushing between my thighs as heat pools.

A voice clears from behind us. "As excited as I am for you, I can't watch my sister like this," Miles says, interrupting our moment.

"Oh shit, man." Gregg places me back down in the soft snow. "I didn't even see you there."

"Who do you think brought the horses down to pick you up? Santa's magic elves?"

Gregg laughs. "Honestly, I can see there being elves on this property."

"Don't give my parents any more ideas," I say, nudging Gregg in the shoulder. The two of us make our way over to Miles and the waiting carriage.

"Seriously, sorry about that. Not exactly how I planned to meet the brother, but it just happened."

Miles introduces himself, sticking his hand out for Gregg to shake. "It's all good. I'm Miles, the best-looking brother and twin." Reaching out, Gregg accepts the handshake. "Gregg."

I stand a few paces behind Gregg as I watch the two men size each other up. It's absolutely barbaric, but being the youngest—and only girl—in a family of four boys, I've come to accept the older brother show. They're all bark and no bite. Even at thirty-one, Miles hasn't changed much.

"Okay, enough," I say before moving past Gregg and jumping into my brother's arms. Squeezing him tight against me, I'm so glad to be home. "I missed you, Brother."

"Missed you too, Sis," Miles says, squeezing me back. "Let's get you two to your cabin before we all freeze to death out here. Gregg, there's a coat for you and extra blankets back there."

I turn to climb the step that leads into the waiting wagon, but not before taking Gregg's outstretched hand. He helps me climb up the three steps and over the ledge. I could climb this wagon with my eyes closed, but I want to relish in this moment with him. He follows after me, the two of us making our way onto the bench seat. Handing Gregg the waiting winter coat, I help him get it on since we are in tight quarters. My heart is warm, even in the cold elements that surround us. The two of us get situated under a patchwork quilt. Once we're cozied together in each other's space, we wait as Miles climbs onto the front driver's bench. With a click of his tongue and a flick of the reins, we watch as the magnificent horses begin to move.

As we make our way up the winding gravel drive to our cabin, I watch as Gregg takes it all in. His eyes bounce from one side to the other as he points out different things along the ride. He really is like a kid on Christmas morning, and I'm so glad I was able to give him this gift of seeing snow. There is nothing better than snow at Christmas time.

"Did Macy tell you that the horses are her favorite part of the property?" Miles asks, shouting over the click-clacking of hooves.

"She hasn't told me too much about growing up here. But it doesn't surprise me that she loves the horses," he answers, glancing over at me.

Miles turns in his seat and lays the reins in his lap so that he's sitting at an angle. He eyes me skeptically, and I shrink under his gaze before he continues. "She used to sneak down to the barn with the carrots Mom would buy. Being out this far from town, groceries were always purchased for a reason, but Macy didn't care. If there were carrots in the fridge, she'd steal them for the horses. One winter, one of the mares was struggling during her pregnancy. She was nearing her due date, and everyone was on labor watch. Macy would get off the bus and head straight to the barn. She'd prop up buckets and make a desk for her to do her homework. Once her homework was out of the way, she'd sit in the stall for hours just reading to the mare. Dad had to practically drag Mace out for supper. If it was up to her, she would've eaten and slept right there next to that mare."

"I would've," I add, fidgeting with my hands in my lap.

"Why does that not surprise me," Gregg whispers so that only I can hear before adding louder for my brother, "She is a nurturer."

"That she is," Miles adds. "So, how long have you two been together?"

My eyes widen at the question. Gregg and I really need to have that discussion. Sooner rather than later, especially before he meets the rest of the brothers. But we aren't about to get into the specifics right here, right now.

Gregg senses my hesitance and wraps his arm around my shoulders, pulling me into his side. "Well," he starts before taking a pause. "We've been—uhh—hanging out since the beginning of school, but, umm—"

"Wait," Miles interrupts, pulling on the reins to stop the horses. Our bodies lurch at the sudden stop. "Are you two just fuck buddies?"

Gregg starts coughing at the same time I yell, "Miles!"

"It's a valid question. I want to know what's going on with the guy my sister is shacking up with."

"It's none of your business what Gregg and I are doing. I seem to remember you having a roster of girls sneaking in and out of your bedroom growing up. Not to mention all the girls that would flock to you after football games. I might be eleven years younger than you, but I grew up in the same house as you."

"Well, I'm a guy, so that's—"

"Don't even think about finishing that sentence, Miles Miller. I will come across this seat and kick your ass."

He laughs. He actually laughs at me. "Oh, I'd like to see you try, little sister." Planting my feet, I stand abruptly, ready to fly over this seat and tackle my brother into the snow. I'm not the tiny little girl I was when we were all living under the same roof. But before I have a chance to attack, Gregg is putting me back in my seat.

"Calm down, Rambo," he says. "And your sister and I are more than just fuck buddies. A lot more."

"Okay, that's enough. We are not doing this whole big brother interrogation bullshit," I say, pointing a glare at my brother. "Just please take us to our cabin."

Miles eyes me for a few awkward moments before clicking his tongue and getting the horses going again.

One brother down, three more to go. Hopefully, my parents keep my brothers away from the cabin so Gregg and I can have a relaxing weekend *reconnecting*.

Chapter 8

Last night was a dream. After my brother finally dropped us off at our cabin, both Gregg and I were ready to shower and relax. Traveling is such a process, not to mention sitting in the airport for two weather delays. I'm just glad we were able to make a flight to Michigan. At one point, I didn't think it was going to happen.

We walked into the cabin to the smell of pizza, the glow of Christmas lights, and the crackling sound of a burning fire. The large A-frame cabin had been recently remodeled. What was once a typical cabin built in the late seventies was now a modernized one. The ceiling still featured wood beams, only they had been updated. White shiplap lined the walls, and the fireplace had been updated with slate stones. Walls had been knocked down, and the entire living space was now one large room. At the back of the living room was a hallway that led to a guest bathroom, a guest bedroom, and the large master suite that ran the entire length of the house.

The two of us ate our pizza in front of the crackling wood fire before falling asleep on the couch. Gregg woke me sometime later, and the two of us moved to the master bedroom. And let's just say, I was amazed at the finishings. The large, four-poster wood bed was made with neutral linens and high thread count sheets. It was like sleeping on a cloud, which is why now, it's nearing ten o'clock, and I am finally getting out of bed.

With one last stretch, I leave the comfort of the ensuite and follow the smell of freshly brewed coffee, which leads me to a shirtless Gregg. He's standing with his back to me, peering out the floor-length windows. The back of this cabin overlooks one of the boat docks on the property. Around the entrance to the lake, trees are scattered all the way to the forest lining the north side of the property. Off the back of the cabin is a wood deck and a small drop-down platform that has a built-in hot tub in the center. From the step-down deck are stairs that meet the stone trails that lead you to the boat dock. Twinkling bistro lights hang above the deck and hot tub. Tall, steel propane heaters are scattered throughout the space. The easily controlled heaters allow warmth to spread over you even on the coldest days. Admiring the view, I'm all too ready to sit out under the stars and twinkling lights while I soak in the hot tub.

Quietly, I move until I'm standing behind Gregg. Lifting my arms, I stretch to wrap myself against him, but before I have a chance, Gregg is reaching his arm behind him, pulling me into his muscled back. He holds me there for a few seconds, both of us enjoying the feel of my cheek resting against his skin. No one moving except for our breaths.

All too quickly, the moment is over, and Gregg spins me to his front. Leaning down, he places a soft kiss on my forehead.

"I didn't think you heard me," I say against his chest.

"I didn't hear you; I could sense you."

"Oh, what? With your Jedi power?" I ask sarcastically, chuckling into his chest.

"Wise one you are," he responds, doing his best Yoda impression.

Laughing, I step out of his arms and take a few steps into the kitchen. I was about to start opening cabinets when a mug on the counter caught my eye. Glancing into the cup, I see that Gregg has already poured creamer inside. Lifting the drink, I take a sniff. Peppermint fills my nostrils, and my heart palpitates. He never ceases to amaze me with gestures that may seem little but make the biggest differences.

"Your mom had it in the fridge," Gregg says from behind me.

With a smile on my face, I pour myself a steaming cup of coffee into the waiting mug of creamer. Spinning around, I rest my back against the counter and blow on the peppermint goodness. Gregg watches me intently. Quirking a brow at him, I wait to see if he's going to share what's on his mind. A slow grin spreads across his face, and in the next moment, he's moving, erasing the space between us. Looking up at him through my lashes, I watch as he bends and places a kiss on my forehead.

"Waffles or French toast?" he murmurs, his lips not leaving my head.

"French toast," I respond.

"You've got it. Now, go sit. Relax, read, do something. Let me cook for you."

With a swat on my butt, he moves past me. I jump at the contact, a small gasp escaping. Adjusting my stance so my legs are crossed at my feet, I watch in wonderment as Gregg goes to the pantry and pulls out a loaf of brioche bread. He moves about the kitchen like he's cooked in here a million times.

"Why are you still standing there?" he asks, not looking up from cracking eggs in a large bowl.

"Did you scope out the kitchen before I woke?"

He shrugs his shoulders as he whisks the eggs with a fork. A fork is a far superior tool to use to whisk eggs, and I love that he knows that. "I *might* have."

Laughing, I turn and glide out of the room, my heart warming at the sight of the man in the kitchen and not from the coffee I'm drinking like it's water.

Fifteen minutes later, Gregg calls from the kitchen to let me know breakfast is ready. Skimming the last couple of lines of my book, I rush to get to a good stopping point. There's nothing worse than stopping in the middle of the chapter. Placing my bookmark in between the pages, I place the closed book on the coffee table and toss off the chunky knit throw blanket.

Glancing toward the breakfast nook that's in the space next to the wall of windows, the sight before me nearly takes my breath away. I was so engrossed in my book that I didn't even hear Gregg moving around behind me. The small nook is set with black and white buffalo plaid placemats, black enameled plates, gold silverware, and white platters filled with French toast, sausage links, and fruit. There's a carafe of orange juice and a bottle of champagne chilling. Waiting. Calling my name.

"What is all of this?" I ask, not keeping the surprise from my voice. Walking into Gregg's outstretched arms, I give him a big squeeze. "This looks perfect."

Stepping out of his embrace, the two of us sit in our chairs. "I wanted to do something special for you," he says. "It's just breakfast, not seeing snow for the first time. But a little something to show how much I appreciate you for planning everything. This trip is one I'll never forget."

"It wasn't that big of a deal," I reply, a blush taking over my face.

His hand finds my thigh, and with a squeeze, he replies, "It was."

His tone is firm and his eyes serious. There's a feeling in the air I can't quite place. A part of me feels like it's love, but the other part of me thinks it's the holiday spirit, and I'm getting my hopes up.

Both of us smile at each other, and I can't help the flutters that make their way from my stomach down to my center. I'm desperate for a connection.

Feeling my face heat, I turn back to the food in front of us, breaking the tension. Reaching into the platter of French toast with the tongs, I grab three pieces. Scooping out butter, I lather the bread and pour a hefty amount of syrup across them. The smell of the sausage has my mouth watering. Gregg places a mimosa in front of me. I take in the pale orange color and know immediately he got the ratio correct—a lot of champagne with a splash of juice.

Cutting a large chunk of the sweet bread, I take a very unladylike bite, moaning around the fork as the taste hits my tongue. I see Gregg pause with his fork halfway to his mouth, his head snapping in my direction. Embarrassment should be what I'm feeling, but I'm way past that. Especially with the way Gregg is staring at the side of my face. My body is turned on. It's pathetic how easily my body comes alive in his presence. My panties shouldn't be this drenched from breakfast and eye contact. But clearly, my body woke up desperate.

"How's your book?" Gregg blurts the question out, causing me to laugh internally at the sudden change.

Chewing my bite, I wait to answer. "It's good, actually. It's like a Gilmore Girls vibe set in winter. These two best friends are forced to fake date each other after a little white lie to enter a competition where the winning money would save and revitalize her Christmas tree farm."

"Well, that sounds interesting."

"It actually is—it's cute and sweet and swoony."

"Swoony?" he asks, quirking a brow.

"Yeah, you know, like, 'awww, so cute.' Romantic. Makes your heart pitter-patter." I describe swooningly while holding my hand over my heart.

He hums at my explanation. "What else makes you pitter-patter?"

Bringing my finger to my mouth, I tap my chin while I think. *I can think of something else that's going pitter-patter right now, and it isn't my heart.*

Taking a gulp of the mimosa, I let the sweet and sour liquid slide down my throat before gesturing to the table in front of me. "This, for starters."

"So this is *swoony*?" Amusement laces his voice.

"Yes, this is swoony," I draw the word out.

Nodding his head, he turns his attention back to the food in front of us.

I think I might die from the sudden whiplash.

Standing in front of the full-length mirror nestled in the corner of the cozy master bedroom, I admire the woman staring back at me. As a little girl, I dreamed of spending Christmas at the cabin with a boy. Some girls wanted Prince Charming in a castle, but I'd dream of my very own Kristoff in the wilderness, the snow around us. Granted, Frozen didn't come out until I was out of the princess stage, but he was the first *real* male lead that I could imagine myself with living the whole "happily ever after" in my very own fairy tale. He was rugged, a little broody, and a blue-collar worker.

I never imagined myself settling down with a preppy guy who expected to be waited on and afraid to get his hands dirty. It's funny because Gregg definitely fits the frat boy persona that a Prince Charming might carry rather than the rugged lumberjack vibes Kristoff had. But he's never flaunted his wealth. He's never shied away from hard work. He's quiet and shy. A bit nerdy but endearing. Compassionate. Dedicated. Hard-working. I thought when I moved to Texas that my dream of spending Christmas in Michigan with a guy was over. But seeing Gregg in this setting, I can picture it. I can picture the happily ever after I've been dreaming of since I was a little girl.

After breakfast, the day quickly melted into the evening as the bright, sunny winter day faded into the most beautiful golden hour, painting the cabin in stunning hues of yellow and orange. My parents arranged for a surprise dinner of steak served with shrimp, mashed potatoes, and roasted vegetables to be sent to our cabin, which we quickly consumed.

Today was the true definition of relaxation as we laid around all day. Gregg watched the CTU basketball game while I read. The snow fell all afternoon in a steady shower, kicking up large scattered squalls, but the fire kept us warm. It felt like we were living in a real-life snow globe.

There's only one thing left for us to do tonight.

Hot tub.

Walking back to the main living space, I pause at the end of the hallway and watch a relaxed Gregg. The room is lit up in a soft orange glow from the fire and the flashing light of the TV. Glancing up from the game recap, Gregg looks in my direction before turning back to the screen. As quickly as he looks away, his gaze captures mine again. I watch his chest rapidly rise and fall. His eyes smolder as his gaze trails a heated path up my legs to my exposed stomach, stopping on the bikini top that leaves little to the imagination, before coming up to meet my eyes, where a seductive smirk curls my lips. I knew picking this tiny red bikini with the triangle-shaped top and very cheeky bottoms was the right choice.

"Holy shit," he rasps, eyes cascading back down my body.

"Hot tub?" I ask. Without replying, Gregg stands from the couch, and in three big strides, he's past me in the direction of the bedroom. I watch as he tugs his shirt over his head with one hand, exposing all of those tight back muscles. Standing there ogling him, I watch as he slides his pants down his legs.

Shaking my head from the lust-filled trance, I quickly escape into the kitchen. Pulling open the fridge, I reach inside and grab a four-pack of local craft beers. Before I head outside, I grab a plastic bowl to fill with snow for a makeshift cooler. The cold, snow-covered deck has me hopping from foot to foot so as not to freeze my toes off. I thumb on the switch to the propane heater that hovers above the hot tub. It's cold out here, but not as freezing as it was last night.

Tapping the buttons, I crank up the bubbles before climbing into the warm water. My body is freezing from the walk to the hot tub. Gliding through the water, I stop in the far corner and prop my arm on the ledge. I stare out over the property, which is lit by the glow of our lights. Our family has made so many memories here, and I'm glad to be back, making more with Gregg.

I hear the back door open and close, but I don't turn around. I just sit with my head resting on my propped arm. The water moves around me as Gregg comes closer. Wrapping his arms around my middle, I feel his chest hit my back, and our bodies relax into each other. Resting his chin on my shoulder, I melt into Gregg's body even more. There's nothing better in the world than skin-to-skin contact.

"Whatcha looking at?" he questions, turning to plant a kiss on my neck, which causes my pulse to quicken.

"Nothing," I answer. Gregg spins us so that he's sitting below me in the built-in seat, and I'm propped on his lap. My legs dangle in the water between his open legs. Wiggling to get comfortable, I start to feel him grow beneath me.

Please don't fight this feeling tonight, Gregg.

"So, about what your brother asked last night," he starts.

"Let's not talk about it." I try to squirm free from his grasp, but his hands tighten around my hips, causing me to still.

"No, we need to talk about it."

"Are we having the *what are we* talk?" I ask, looking straight ahead and avoiding his gaze.

"Don't you think it's time?" he ponders.

With a nod, I wait for him to begin. His hands flex—one remaining around my waist while the other settles on the inside of my thigh. The movement causes me to squirm against his lap—again. Gregg lets out a hiss from between his teeth at the connection.

"The last few weeks have been great," Gregg begins. At his words, my chest tightens as the anxiety creeps in. Is Gregg seriously about to break up with me? Who starts a conversation off with such an ominous tone? "But I feel like you were forced into this situation."

"I wasn't forced into anything," I interrupt. My lungs feel like they could explode from the heaviness of his tone. "I wouldn't have offered to move in with you if I didn't want to or if I didn't think it was the right thing to do."

Is this seriously happening right now? Is Gregg going to dump me while we are sitting half-naked in a hot tub one thousand miles away from our apartment?

"Right, that's exactly it." I watch as his head turns to the side, his eyes glued to our surroundings. "You just said it was the right thing to do. And you're a great person, the best. But I just feel like everything between us shifted so fast. Especially with my parents calling you my girlfriend. Which, by the way, I never called you."

"Gregg, what are you trying to say? You're starting to freak me out."

He lets out an exasperated sigh, and all I want to do is climb off his lap and melt into the snow around us. "I'm not trying to freak you out. Why are words so hard?"

Reaching up, I hesitantly place my hand on the side of his face, his stubble poking into the palm of my hand, turning it so that he is forced to face me. "Just say what's on your mind. If you want whatever this is to end between us, then just spit it out."

"Shit, Mace. That's not what I'm trying to say at all."

"Well, you sure had me fooled," I grumble. Resting his forehead on my shoulder, I feel his breath slide across my skin, causing goosebumps to prickle across my body even though we are surrounded by hot water. I feel my nipples harden into peaks and hope he doesn't notice. *Or maybe he should notice and remember how much fun we have together.*

"What I'm trying to say is that the last few weeks have been incredible. You are the most beautiful, most selfless person I know. You dropped everything to move in with me. To help a near stranger recover from a life-threatening stroke. You amaze me every single day. We were just supposed to be a one-time thing, but I knew there was something more between us. I guess what I'm trying to say is that I'm in love with you. I know it seems fast, but everything about our relationship has been fast and done out of order. But at the end of the day, I've realized that life is short, and I don't want to waste any more time of us going through the motions. I want us to be official—exclusive—whatever the right thing to call us is. I don't want us to be *just* roommates. I want us to share a bed, the apartment to feel like our home, and eventually build a life together."

Before Gregg has a chance to catch his breath from rushing his words out, my lips are crashing into his. I didn't know how badly I needed to hear those words until they came pouring from his lips. It's not even the declaration that he loves me—*oh my gosh, Gregg* loves *me*—but the declaration he wants more between us.

A future. A life. Forever.

My heart feels like it's going to beat through my chest. I feel his erection below me, which only spurs me on.

Breaking our kiss, I turn in his arms, bringing my legs to straddle his waist. The movement causes my center to line up perfectly with his growing cock. Sitting up straighter, I dive my hands in his hair, causing his head to tilt back. My movements don't stop until I get him where I want him. I angle his head to my advantage as I deepen our kiss. Our tongues tangle, each one of us fighting to get the upper hand.

His taste is intoxicating. It's a drug I crave.

Gregg's hands skate up my back, pulling me in closer. Our bodies are squished together, with no space separating us. With a slight tug, I feel the strings of my bikini top loosen from the middle of my back. His hand continues to climb. Gripping the nape of my neck, he pulls the strings loose, causing the bubbles to force my bikini to float away and leaving my chest completely exposed.

In one swift motion, Gregg is standing from his seat, causing my legs to wrap around his waist. The exposed cold air causes my nipples to harden past the point I thought was possible. They are so hard they hurt. They ache with the need of his touch. The only thing that will soothe them.

He glides us through the water. Bending down, he finds one pebbled nipple and sucks it between his teeth. He bites down, and I let out a loud, long moan, desperate for more. Placing me on the edge of the hot tub, he takes a step back. Our chests heave, the tension of what's to come lingering between us. I watch as his gaze sets my body on fire, and suddenly, the chill in the air is gone.

"I've missed your body," he rasps. "Do you trust me?"

"Yes," I reply without any hesitation. In the next breath, Gregg is in front of me, hands finding the ties of my bottoms. In seconds, he has my bottoms removed, and I'm sitting on the edge of the hot tub, completely naked. The blast of cold air quickly subsides as the heat from the heater warms my wet skin.

"Spread," he demands.

My legs part at his harsh words. I know the exact moment he sees the glisten giving away how wet I am. His pupils darken as his tongue comes out to run across his bottom lip. I've never been jealous of a tongue, but oh, how I wish I was the one running my tongue against his lip.

Squatting into the water, Gregg grips my legs as his mouth dives into my pussy. His tongue finds my center, and with one thick stroke, he has me moaning for more. Rocking my pussy across his tongue, his light stubble creates a friction I desperately crave. I carefully buck against him, begging for more. With a flick of his tongue against my clit, I can't fight the moan that erupts from me.

He pulls away, and I groan in frustration. Forest green eyes find mine. "Damn, baby, you're dripping."

"More," I beg. I feel his chuckle as his face finds my center again. He laps at my dripping pussy. Throwing my head back, I do little to keep quiet. The louder I moan, the more Gregg reacts to my response. It doesn't take long before I feel the tightness in my lower belly, my orgasm building.

I'm so focused on chasing my high that I don't notice Gregg's hand has disappeared from the water. His mouth leaves me, and I groan, again, at the loss of his touch. Before I have a chance to object, my center is met with something cold.

I gasp at the temperature change. Looking down, I see a glob of white covering me. "Did you just put snow on my pussy?" I choke out. Shivers run down my spine as goosebumps line my skin.

The cold snow changes my temperature immediately, causing my nipples to harden to the point of pain yet again. Before I can jump in the water to warm up, Gregg's mouth is back on me, his tongue lapping away the snow. The hot and cold create a new sensation that has that familiar feeling swelling in the pit of my stomach. Gregg plunges two fingers inside of me, curling them up and working that spot deep inside me.

In seconds I'm coming. Wetness drips from me, but Gregg doesn't let up. My head tilts back, my arms shaking. Gregg's other hand is the only assurance I have from toppling over as I scream out my release. Glancing down, I find his gaze watching me come undone. He continues assaulting my clit in a fast, dizzying movement as I come down from the earth-shattering orgasm I've been desperately waiting for. Toys just don't get the job done.

Pulling back from me, I watch Gregg's hooded gaze as I see myself glistening around his mouth. I continue my perusal of his bare chest, admiring the definition of his abs. My eyes find his erection jutting toward me. A small gasp escapes as I'm quickly reminded of how *big* Gregg is, even underneath his trunks. All I can think about is what it would be like to come with that inside of me. I miss the feel of his cock as it stretches me wide. His demanding voice has my pussy fluttering as if she didn't come seconds ago. He has my pussy turning into a needy hussy.

"Turn around," Gregg gives another demand. Without hesitation, I turn around. Coming up behind me, Gregg pushes my back down until my breasts are resting on the ledge and my ass is in the air, thanks to the seat I'm standing on. I'm fully exposed and in such a vulnerable position, but I have never been more turned on in my life.

Gregg's tongue finds me from behind, and I moan as he tastes my clit. Just as quickly as he appears, his mouth is gone, replaced with his fingers. With a few quick pumps, I feel Gregg sidle up behind me. Glancing over my shoulder, I watch as he takes the hand that's not inside of me and tugs his swim trunks down. His cock springs free, and my mouth goes dry. A cocky smirk finds Gregg's face as he watches me watch him.

I've never been more thankful for our height differences than I am right now. Removing his fingers, I feel his length line up to my center before he enters me in one quick thrust.

Both of us groan at the sensation. I feel my walls clench around his length, causing Gregg to suck in a breath. He's big and so thick. My body feels like she's being split in half. The burning pain quickly turns into pleasure. It's been months since he's been inside of me.

"You've got to relax, or this is going to be over very quickly. Even at that, I might not last. It's been a long time, and you feel so fucking good," he grits out. After a few seconds, my body adjusts to his size, and he's thrusting into me. His hips hit my ass, and it feels incredible.

The sounds. The sensation. The sensory overload has me on the brink of bliss.

With one hand tightly gripping my hip, his other hand slips around to the front of me. He finds my clit immediately as if they're connected by magnets.

Rubbing hard, tight circles, I notice the familiar feeling start to build in my lower belly again. My spine tingles at the anticipation of the explosion that is about to take place. "I'm going to come," I pant out.

"I know," he grits. "You're so fucking tight."

And with a few more circles around my clit, I cry out as euphoria takes over. Gregg thrusts one, two, three more times before he's quickly sliding out of me. I glance over my shoulder as I watch him stroke himself before hot, white streams land over my ass. His come coats my exposed skin, and I revel in the warmth. Both of us collapse as the overwhelming feeling hits us.

Standing up, Gregg reaches over the side of the hot tub and finds his t-shirt. I feel the material on my skin as he wipes his pleasure from my back.

"Fuck," he pants, tossing the shirt back to the ground. "You're so perfect."

Turning around, I wrap my arms around him, pushing him backward into the water. My lips find his. Pulling away, my lids are heavy as I look at him in a blissed-out, post-orgasm daze.

"I love you."

Chapter 9

"**A**re you ready for this?"

Gregg and I are standing outside of the lodge, where we have plans to meet my family for breakfast. It's Gregg's first time meeting my family—aside from Miles, and that wasn't the best welcome.

"I'm fine, babe. Stop worrying." He bends down and places a kiss on my lips before stomping off the loose snow from his boots. After our steamy hot tub session, a mini snowstorm dropped off a couple more inches while I was busy getting a few—or a lot—of inches, too.

It turns out the hot tub session was just the beginning of our night. After going for so long without sex, Gregg planned on making it up to me last night—and early this morning. My body is exhausted and sore from being bent and twisted into so many positions. But the few hours of sleep I managed was the best sleep of my life. I was thoroughly sated.

Pushing open the door, I stomp my feet on the welcome rug before following Gregg inside. The lodge is a massive building on our property. The vaulted, wood beam ceiling makes the entrance feel grand while the lighting gives a warm glow, especially at night. A front desk greets you, and the walkway pushes you into the open space. A floor-to-ceiling back wall exposes the entire wooded property. A stone fireplace runs the height of the walls and is centered between the windows. Brown leather couches and chairs are spread throughout the room, inviting guests to sit and relax—and escape the confines of their cabin.

Half of the lodge is set up for dining with a mixture of rectangular and circular tables and leather back chairs surrounding them. The restaurant in the lodge is open from six in the morning until nine at night. The bar offers specialty cocktails and local craft beers, as well as a variety of pre-made snacks that are available while the lodge is open.

Christmastime inside the lodge is my favorite. Pine garland and red ribbon line every inch of the space. Every year my dad goes out to the woods with the horses and a wagon. He seeks out the best evergreen tree to cut down—typically around sixteen feet tall. My mom always has the tree decorated with white lights, red and gold baubles, and a giant star on top. It's magical and always takes my breath away. The tables have red runners that accent all the maroon details sprinkled throughout the lodge. Pine wreaths hang from the large windows, and the snowy backdrop makes you feel like you're stepping into a painting.

"Ah, there she is!" I turn toward the squealing voice that echoes in the open space. A wide smile breaks across my face as I move toward my mom. She's rushing to us from the largest rectangular table that sits in the center of the dining space. Which is also full of my family. Throwing her arms around me, she grabs me in a strong, loving embrace. "My baby is home!"

"Hi, Mom," I say, squeezing her back. There's no better feeling than having your mom wrap you in an embrace. I know it's been killing her to wait to see us, but I appreciate that she gave Gregg and me the space we needed to relax.

She pulls back and holds me out at arm's length, taking in my appearance. "Oh, sweetie, you look so wonderful. You're practically glowing."

My cheeks flame at her words. Can she tell that her daughter just had orgasm after orgasm last night? And spent the morning getting fucked all over the cabin?

Gregg smothers a laugh behind me, no doubt thinking what I'm thinking.

With one last long look at my face, she turns to Gregg. "Gregg!" she exclaims, pulling him into a hug. "It's so good to finally meet you!"

He hugs her back like they are long-lost friends. "It's wonderful to meet you too, Mrs. Miller. Although it feels like we met a long time ago."

She pulls out of his grasp and gives him a swat. "Please. Call me Dana. That lady over there," she gestures over her shoulder. I chuckle as I'm reminded of a familiar conversation with Gregg's mom. "That's Mrs. Miller. And FaceTime doesn't count, dear."

Both of our gazes go back to the overwhelming amount of people at the table. That's when I notice my grandparents are also gathered around the table. Grumbling under my breath, I say, "I didn't know this was going to be a whole family meeting."

"I didn't know it was going to be either," she responds, rolling her eyes. "Come. Come. Cook will have breakfast out soon."

She turns, leading Gregg and me to the firing squad. I mean my family. "I'm sorry for the ambush."

"Would you stop apologizing? I promise I'm fine," Gregg says. I feel his hand brush mine before he's gripping it, sliding his fingers through mine. With a gentle squeeze, I glance at the contact before meeting his gaze. He gives me a subtle wink, causing me to grin. He's right; it's fine. It's just my family. Four older, overprotective brothers, my parents, and my grandparents. What could possibly go wrong?

To my surprise, breakfast goes smoothly. Once Gregg and I were seated at the table, I didn't have a chance to introduce everyone before Cook brought out platters of food. Scrambled eggs, breakfast meats, hash browns, pancakes, fruit, and everything in between lined our table. It was enough food to feed the entire CTU football team. I would know—Brynn, Chloe, and I would host weekly "family" dinners. The girls and I would spend all day Sunday cooking homemade meals and feeding all of our friends. It was the perfect way to wrap up the weekend before the hectic schedules resumed at the start of the week.

I take one last bite of the strawberry on my plate before pushing it out of the way. I can't manage another bite. Leaning back, I stretch in my chair before patting my very full stomach. "I'm stuffed," I say. "Everything was delicious, like always."

"Thanks, dear. Cook is the best cook around," my dad boasts. Pride is evident in his voice. The restaurant inside the lodge was something that he started when he took over operations. It started out small, only offering a breakfast buffet and meals for special occasions. But it quickly turned into a local landmark that many tourists—and locals—frequent.

"Wait," Gregg says, pausing. "Your cook's name is Cook?"

I laugh. "Yes. His name is Aaron Cook. He went to school with Carter and always went by his last name, so it just stuck. It's pretty ironic he became a cook."

"Which one is Carter?" Gregg whispers in my ear.

"Oh yeah, let me introduce everyone." Realizing I haven't made introductions since I briefly said hello, I stand from my chair, moving to the person right next to me. "You've already met Miles," I say with an eye roll.

Miles looks toward Gregg and gives him a head nod. I think it's the universal way guys say hello.

Moving next to Miles, I introduce the next person. "This is my Grandpa Miller and my Grandma Miller. They ran the Cozy Cabin until Dad took it over twenty-five years ago."

Sliding behind my grandparents, I kiss them both on the cheeks. "This is Mason," I shout back to Gregg. "He's worse than Miles, so be warned. And this is Sarah, his girlfriend." Walking around the table, I find my favorite brother. Before I have a chance to introduce him, he's standing and embracing me in his big brother bear hug, squeezing me so hard I can barely breathe as my feet dangle in the air.

"Okay," I groan. "I can't breathe you ogre."

"But I missed my favorite sister," he says.

"I'm your only sister," I grit out.

He places me back on my feet and turns back to Gregg. "I'm Max, Menace's favorite. I also know all of her secrets. Before you leave, get my number and I'll hook you up."

Backhanding him in the stomach, my brother groans at the contact. "You will not be doing that."

Max just smiles down at me. "It's good having you home, Menace."

I groan at the nickname Max gave me when we were kids. I can't remember what caused him to call me Menace, but once he did, it just kind of stuck.

Pulling me in for a normal hug, he whispers so only I can hear him. "I've missed you."

"Missed you, too." I squeeze him back. The two of us release each other, and I move on to my last brother. "Last and certainly not least, this is Carter. The first Miller son and the wildest. Although, we have his wife, Jessica, to thank for finally calming his crazy ass down."

"Mom, Aunt Macy said ass," my nephew whines to his mom.

"Yes, she did. But what have I told you about saying adult words?" Jessica scolds.

"But Aunt Macy said it first."

"And she's an adult," Jessica says.

"Oops, sorry," I apologize to Carter and Jessica, wincing.

"It's fine," Carter says. "We've been trying to teach Noah that adults can say adult words and that when he hears them, he shouldn't *repeat* the word when he tattles."

Noah slides down in his chair—either from embarrassment or he's trying to hide. Walking past Carter, I lean down and give Jessica a small hug before moving on to my nephew.

Squatting down so that I'm at eye level with Noah, I lean in and whisper, "Sorry buddy, I didn't mean to get you in trouble."

"It's fine," he mumbles.

"I'd like to introduce you to someone special." I point over toward Gregg.

"Is that your boyfriend?" he asks.

I nod my head. "Yes, that's Gregg. Gregg, this is my super cool, super ornery nephew, Noah."

"Hey, Noah," Gregg greets with a warm smile.

Noah eyes him for a beat before he turns to me. "He's cool. I like him," he says, shrugging like it's no big deal, causing everyone around the table to laugh.

"I'm glad he got the Noah Miller approval." I stand, kissing him on the forehead before ruffling his hair. I move on to the princess sitting between Noah and my mom. Bending down, I kiss the top of her head in rapid succession, tickling her side as I introduce her. "And this cutie is Rachel."

Rachel is two, and she is rotten. Being only the second girl in our family, my parents have spoiled her to no end. Right now, food is smeared all over her face and hands. I leave her in her high chair. I'll play with her once her mom gets her cleaned. That's one of the perks of aunt duty: you can leave the messes for their parents.

I finish the walk around the table and sit back in my chair. Gregg wraps his arm around my shoulders, pulling me in closer to him.

"There's going to be a pop quiz before you leave," Miles says from the other side of me.

"Yeah, try not to get the M names mixed up," Max shouts from the end of the table. Everyone laughs. Mason, Miles, Max, Macy—it is a mouthful to remember. Carter is lucky to be named after our great-grandfather. Somewhere along the way, the first-born son is named after another male in our family. It's a bit archaic, but not a tradition I see ending anytime soon. I have no idea why they tortured themselves by naming the rest of us 'm' names. Even as the only girl, I can't tell you how many times I got called one of my brothers' names.

Silence falls over the table. Jessica takes that as her cue to gather her kids and take them to get cleaned up. My grandpa stands from his seat and walks toward the leather sofa that sits in front of the fireplace, and my grandma follows. Max, Mason, and Carter stand from their seats and find empty spots closer to us. Mom rolls her eyes before standing to give one of my brothers her seat. She knows the Miller interrogation is about to start.

"So, Gregg. Macy tells us you're on the golf team," my dad says, turning his attention to Gregg.

Taking a sip of his water, Gregg answers. "Yes, this is my third year. Well, it was supposed to be."

"Why golf?" Max asks.

"Why not golf?" Carter asks Max. "What's wrong with golf?"

"I didn't say anything was wrong with it. It's just not a common sport."

"It actually is. I golf every weekend," Mason chimes in.

Miles scoffs. "I wouldn't call what you do golf. More like you get wasted and ride around on a golf cart."

"Eh, it's all the same in my book," Mason says.

"Boys, enough," my dad scolds. "I swear, you'd think once you all turned thirty, you'd quit the childish behavior."

Max scoffs. "How dare you, Dad. I'm not thirty."

My dad just shakes his head, muttering something incoherent under his breath as he turns his attention back to Gregg. "How did you get started with golf?"

"My dad, actually. His firm does a lot of deals on the golf course. I would go with him when I was little and when he'd go to the driving range. Turns out I had skill at a young age, and we just kept working on it. CTU came calling my senior year, and I accepted a scholarship. I never thought I'd be playing in college, but here I am."

"Any plans to go pro?" Carter asks.

Gregg sighs, taking another sip of his water. "I honestly don't even know if I'll be able to finish out my career."

I squeeze Gregg's leg as a somber mood falls on the table. Out of the corner of my eye, I watch Max lean into Carter, and his whisper can be heard. "Nice job, asshole."

I snap my head to both of them, glaring at them to shut the hell up. I love my brothers to pieces, but sometimes they can be real jackasses. "It's fine," Gregg whispers in my ear as he squeezes my hand, which is resting on his thigh.

"How are you feeling?" Miles asks. "You really freaked my sister out."

"Miles!" I shout. Frustration boils inside of me. I knew my brothers would be concerned and a bit difficult, but they're all acting like assholes.

"I'm doing well. The recovery has been challenging, but the physical therapy has been doing wonders on my left side. The cold hasn't helped anything, but it's just part of the process. I don't know if my golf game will be as good as it was, but we'll see."

"Wait," I interject, snapping my head in Gregg's direction before I turn to look at his left hand that's hanging off my shoulder. Reaching up, I grab his hand and examine it before looking at Gregg. "You didn't tell me the cold was bothering your hand."

"It's fine," Gregg says, leaning in to brush his lips against my temple in a sweet, barely there kiss. "The hot tub helped."

My cheeks burn, and I immediately divert my gaze to my coffee mug. I have no doubt if I look up, at least one of my brothers will figure out the hidden meaning behind Gregg's words. I only pray no one heard us last night.

Miles leans into my other side. "You know I heard this really weird sound coming from your cabin's side of the property," he whispers in my ear. With a sideways glance at Miles, I reach for my mug of coffee. Gregg, Carter, and my dad continue their conversation while Miles tries to get me to acknowledge him.

"I thought you said you two were more than just fuck buddies," he grits through his teeth.

Sinking down in my chair, I start to push away from the table, causing Gregg to remove his arm. He looks over at me, and I give him a reassuring smile before getting up and walking away from the table. Footsteps follow me, and I have no doubt that Miles and Max are behind me. I continue walking until I reach the opposite end of the lodge. Turning on my heels, I unleash.

"What's your problem with Gregg?" I snap at Miles.

"I have a problem with you dropping everything for some guy who just looks at you as a hookup."

"How dare you," I start, gritting my teeth. "You have no idea what goes on in Texas. I'm not sixteen anymore, Miles. I can take care of myself."

"I'm still your older brother, and I will step in when I think that my sister isn't being treated fairly. You dropped your townhouse, and your friends, to what? Play nurse to some rich kid?"

"He almost died," I all but yell at him, turning the attention of a few nearby guests.

"Would you two knock it off?" Max steps in. "I think what Miles is trying to say is that we love you, Sis. We just want to make sure that you are happy and okay."

"Well, I am. I'm in love with Gregg, and he loves me, too." I internally roll my eyes at how much of a girl I sound like.

"Holy shit, bro," Max gasps. "Our little sister is in *love*."

I glare at Max. He's always such a clown.

"You mean that? It's more than just a casual hookup?" Miles asks, his eyes bouncing back and forth, trying to get a read on me.

"Yes, Miles," I sigh, smiling up at my big brother. "We love each other. We're exclusive. Now please stop with the interrogations."

"If he ever hurts you," Miles says, a seriousness taking over his tone.

"I know," I smile wider. "You'll be my first call to kick his ass."

"Noted." I hear over my brothers' shoulders. I didn't see Gregg walk up, what with my brothers towering over me and creating a wall. He reaches out a hand to Miles. "I promise to protect her and treat her right."

Miles eyes Gregg's hand, drawing out the moment. Finally, he reaches out and shakes Gregg's palm. Before letting go, he pulls him in for what looks like an awkward guy hug. "And please, for the love of all things, don't screw my sister outside where her family can hear her."

I watch as the color drains from Gregg's face as mine heats.

"Oh God, that was *you*?" Max asks. "I need to go clean my ears."

I have never felt more embarrassed in my life.

Chapter 10

Christmas week is finally here. I think it's safe to say Gregg is no longer Mr. Scrooge. On our flight home yesterday afternoon, I overheard him humming a Christmas carol. It was like seeing a deer; I made sure to make no sudden movements so I didn't scare him off.

This morning I came out to the living room to find presents wrapped under the tree. I'm not sure when he found the time to do them, but seeing them made our tiny apartment feel like a home. It might have been the exhaustion from our quick long weekend in Michigan, or that we finally had a discussion about our relationship, but when my head hit the pillow, I slept so peacefully. Or maybe it was because I finally moved into Gregg's room, and the two of us slept wrapped in each other's arms. My mind was finally able to shut off, allowing me to get a full night's sleep.

Being back home was the refresher I needed. The last couple of months have been challenging, and I didn't realize I was harboring so much stress. But being at the cabin, shutting out the world around us, I felt like I was finally able to breathe. Even my mom could see the change. We might not get to see each other as often as we both would like, but FaceTime helps. She's noticed the dark circles below my eyes over the last few months, especially the weeks right after Gregg's stroke.

Those days are ones I never want to relive. I have never been so scared in my entire life. Watching the person I was falling for lay in a hospital bed with tubes and wires hooked to him was the most traumatizing thing I've ever faced. It took a while for the nightmares to stop. So many nights, I'd wake up in a cold sweat after a horrible nightmare where Gregg wouldn't survive. On those nights, I'd get up and creep out of my room to check on him. I'd stand in his doorway and watch him sleep. Yes, I know how creepy that sounds, but it gave me peace of mind. I could see him. I could see he was still alive and still breathing. Gregg was still there with me.

I haven't had a nightmare in a week, and it's all because of his improvement. I only hope that his being in the cold didn't make all of his progress disappear. I still can't believe he didn't tell me the cold weather was affecting him.

"Where'd you go, beautiful?" Gregg asks as he sits down on the couch beside me. Nestling into him, I inhale his scent—pine and eucalyptus. For a man who hasn't enjoyed Christmas in the past, he sure always smells like Christmas. I don't think he realizes his cologne is made up of a few signature holiday scents.

"Nowhere," I answer. Burdening Gregg with my thoughts and nightmares isn't worth the trouble. He has enough to worry about. "Ready to bake cookies?"

"Do we have to?" he asks with a groan.

"I'll compromise with you. We'll make one batch of cookies, and then we can cuddle on the couch."

"Hmm, that sounds like a benefit for you. Baking and cuddling? Do you always make deals where you benefit from both outcomes?"

I twist my lips to the side, mulling over another thought. "Cuddling without clothes?"

"Deal," he says, jumping up out of his seat, causing me to flop where he was just holding me. "Hurry up, woman. We've got cookies to bake."

My laugh fills the air.

These are the moments we'll remember forever.

Giggling, I reach over and wipe the flour from Gregg's cheek. We've been baking for an hour, and I think more flour has ended up on the floor or on Gregg than in the batter. The kitchen has been filled with laughter all afternoon as we mix the batter, roll out the dough, cut cookies in various Christmas shapes, and line our counters with cooling racks.

"How does the flour keep getting everywhere?" Gregg groans as he looks down at his black sweatpants, which are covered in flour.

Chuckling, I toss him a wet washcloth. "I've never met such a hot mess when it comes to baking."

"It's not my fault," he pleads. "My mom wasn't a baker."

Leaning on my tiptoes, I wrap my arms around his neck, pulling him closer to me. Sticking my tongue out, I lick his cheek, cleaning the flour from his face.

"Macy Marie," he groans, squeezing me into his body.

"What?" I question, feigning innocence.

Shaking his head, he pulls away. "Let's get this mess cleaned up, and then I'll let you order Chinese for dinner."

Quirking a brow, I plant my hand on my hip. "Oh, you'll *let me* order Chinese food."

"Yep," he answers, turning to grab a mixing bowl.

"Let me do the cleanup," I say, taking the bowl from him and walking it to the sink. He follows me, wrapping his arms around me from behind. Resting his head on my shoulder, he nuzzles my neck. Nuzzling quickly turns into kissing and nibbling the space where my neck meets my shoulder. I lean into the kisses, feeling his effect on my lower back. Groaning, I roll my neck away from his kisses.

"Go shower. Let me clean the kitchen."

With one last peck on my cheek, Gregg slaps my ass before striding out of the room. My gaze lingers in the doorway even after he's long gone. Shaking my head, I grab my phone to place our Chinese order from the takeout place down the street. I love that Gregg's apartment is next to my favorite Chinese restaurant—the one that always has our order ready in ten minutes. Once our dinner is ordered, I turn back to the mess of dirty dishes that linger.

Today's baking session has been the messiest one I've ever experienced. Batter is stuck to the ceiling after a major mixer incident. Flour is sprinkled all over the flour, again after a major mixer incident. And every bowl we have is dirty.

Who knew Santa's simple sugar cookies would be such a disaster?

I'm twisting the lock on the front door, arms full of the Chinese food that was just delivered, as Gregg emerges from the bathroom. "Mmm, just in time." Walking over, he takes the bag of Chinese from my hands and carries it over to our coffee table. I love that he shares the same joy of Chinese food at the coffee table as I do. There's just something about eating from the cardboard boxes right there in the living room. I detour into the kitchen to grab our wine glasses.

"Here, babe," I say, handing Gregg his glass of Riesling. He stops rustling through the bags, pulling out crab rangoon, egg rolls, fried rice, and Kung Pao Chicken.

"Good choice on the food," he says, getting comfortable on the couch.

Sliding between him and the coffee table, I, too, make myself comfortable. Reaching for the remote, I push play on the movie I already had queued up. The introduction scenes of *Office Christmas Party* fill the screen.

"This is the Christmas movie you picked?"

My lips curl upward at his excited voice. "I thought you might like it," I say around a bite full of food.

The two of us settle into our meals as we watch Jason Bateman plan an all-out office Christmas party.

With only six days until the big day, I think we've made the most of the seasonal activities. We've decorated a tree together, curled up with Christmas movies, exchanged ornaments, looked at Christmas lights, gone Christmas shopping, sat on Santa's lap, enjoyed cocktails while watching people ice skate, visited a cabin in the winter, experienced Gregg's first snow together, and had hot tub sex. After tonight, Gregg can cross *baking Christmas cookies* off the list of things he never got to do as a kid.

Reliving all these memories with Gregg has made this December one I will always remember.

"YOU HAVE A FRESHLY FUCKED AURA."

"**I** think you've officially lost your mind," Gregg yells over the very loud, very off-key singing coming from the speakers. He glances around the packed bar and shakes his head.

The Eagles Nest is a campus staple. The bar is known for its wings, cheap beer, ladies' night, and themed events. Every year, the bar hosts a karaoke night on the night before Christmas Eve. But tonight, tonight is a special holiday night. Anyone wearing a Christmas outfit got in for free. I found Gregg a super obnoxious Christmas sweatshirt that had a giant cat across the chest saying *Meowy Christmas*. I promised him that others would be wearing ugly Christmas sweaters, too. It was the only way I could convince him to leave the apartment. Well, not the only way. I did bribe him with sexual favors afterward.

Glancing around the bar, it's hard to find anyone as a sea of people sway to the guy singing on stage. He's terrible, but I'm not one to make fun because standing in front of people singing is my literal worst fear.

"There's Brynn," Gregg shouts, pointing in the direction of a booth in the back corner, opposite the stage. He steps in front of me, and I take his hand in mine as I follow. He's parting the crowd like the Red Sea.

"Merry Christmas Eve Eve," I greet our group of friends.

"You two finally fucked!" Brynn shouts, causing people to look our way. My cheeks flame as she bounces up and down in her seat with excitement.

Quinton shakes his head, used to his no-filter girlfriend.

"Yes, Brynn. You know we have," I respond, sliding into the booth next to Grant. He's the football coach's son and one of Quinton's closest friends.

"No, no. Like recently. You have a freshly fucked aura," she says, waving her hands around the air.

Gregg smirks, pulling a bottle of Coors Light from the bucket in front of us.

"I didn't know that was a type of aura," Grant goads from beside me.

"Oh yeah, it totally is. It's like a giant arrow pointing down on her saying she's in a state of orgasmic bliss."

"An orgasmic bliss?" Quinton laughs at her description. "I think you've had too much to drink, Wilder."

With a flick of her wrist, she reaches forward and grabs another beer. "Or have I not had enough to quiet my wild brain?"

Reaching in for the last beer, I twist the cap off, holding it out for Brynn. "I'll drink to that," I say as we clink bottles.

"I thought you said the guys would all be wearing *ugly* Christmas sweaters." Gregg points at Quinton with his beer bottle. Q's wearing a navy and red trimmed sweater with a winter design lined horizontally across the chest. In the center is the Captain America emblem.

"I told Wilder there was no way I was wearing *something like that*," Quinton quips back, laughing at Gregg's cat sweater.

"But Captain America is the weakest superhero," Grant adds.

Shaking my head, I add, "But he's the hottest."

"You take that back!" Brynn says. "Thor is by far the hottest," she purrs, running her tongue across her lip before pulling it in her mouth, a smirk lining her lips.

"Want us to give you a minute, Wilder," Quinton quips.

Looking around, Brynn responds, "Why? Is Chris Hemsworth in the bar?"

The table erupts in laughter. Quinton and Brynn's banter never ceases to make me laugh. The two are perfect for each other.

"All I'm saying is," Brynn starts before taking a pull of her beer. "When you get in the NFL, you better figure out how to get Chris Hemsworth to attend one of your games so I can meet him."

"Yeah," Q laughs. "Like hell, that's going to happen."

Flopping back in her seat, she folds her arms around her chest as her face pulls into a pout. I toss my napkin at her. It hits her in the face. Her eyes snap in my direction, and we both burst out in laughter.

"Is it just the five of us tonight?" I ask, trying to control my hysterics.

"Oh no, JP is around here somewhere," Brynn answers as the DJ announces JP is up next. JP is Jeremiah Prince, but everyone calls him by his nickname. He's a defensive back on the football team.

"Woo, JP!" Brynn shouts as the rest of us yell out encouraging cheers.

Making his way on the stage, we watch as JP gets comfortable in front of the crowd. Clearing his throat in the microphone, the music to Run DMC's "Christmas in Hollis" starts playing. Everyone gets up, including our table, as we all try to find space on the floor.

"Yeah, JP!" Q bellows in his cupped hands.

With a hand on my hip, Gregg moves me so that I'm situated in front of him, gripping my sides and pulling me tighter into him.

My ass rests against the zipper of his jeans. Swaying my hips against his front, I let the rhythm of the song control my movements. Gregg's grip tightens even more as our bodies move to the beat of the song. I feel him grow harder against my ass, and I can't help the smile that breaks free. It's sensual, methodical, our own version of foreplay at what's to come when we get home. Looking up over my shoulder, I see a wide grin across Gregg's face, too, and I know that coming here tonight was a great idea. I only hope he's not too upset with me after he sees the surprise I have in store for him.

The crowd loses it as JP wraps up the song. His personality mixed with this song was a deadly combination that surprised no one. JP's not-so-hidden talent is that he loves to bust out in raps. He might not be the next up-and-coming rapper, but he knows how to drop a beat. "Yo, Macy," JP draws out through the microphone. "You're up, girl."

Dread pools in my stomach. I knew Gregg would only get up and sing if I did, so I texted Brynn earlier and had her put me on the list. Tonight I'm living my worst fear for the man I love.

Stepping out of Gregg's arms, I make my way to the stage. People pat me on the shoulder and shout encouragements as I weave through the crowd.

You've got this. You've got this.

With a deep inhale, I climb up the few steps that lead me out onto the stage. Raising my hand, I use it to block out the bright light from the spotlight. *Why is it so bright?* JP meets me with his fist out, waiting for me to bump it.

Hitting my fist with his, he whispers, "You've got this," and then walks off the stage.

The opening notes to "Santa Tell Me," Ariana Grande's version, starts, and I watch the screen in front of me, waiting for my cue to start singing. Reading the lyrics, I let the song flow through my veins. The music takes me to a new place as my body begins to move with the beat.

As much as I hate singing in public, I can't deny that I have a pretty decent voice. I've been singing in the church choir since I was in junior high. It was the *only* public place I sang. There was no way I was opening myself up to the criticism of my classmates in high school.

Emotion washes through me as the words pour from my soul. The song is about a new love and asking Santa if this guy really cares about me. The crowd quiets as my voice filters through the space. I knew I had a good voice—a great voice—but quieting a bar of drunk college students shocks me.

Letting the final lyrics pour from my mouth, I feel the moisture welling up in my eyes. My heart beats at the overflowing amount of emotion. At this moment, my heart feels full. The love Gregg and I share is real. It's the kind of love I've been searching for. I finally feel like I've kissed my last toad, and Gregg Carlton is the one for me.

He's my future.

I've never felt so seen, so appreciated, and so adored as I do with him. We might not have started in the most conventional way, but the love that has grown and flourished is truly something people wish for.

Clapping erupts throughout the bar, bringing me back to the moment. A smile breaks free, and I bend over as laughter wracks through me. Standing back up, I wave at the crowd. Then, slowly, I turn away, feeling like I'm walking on a cloud, when two large hands enclose my face. Soft lips meet mine in a searing kiss. I gasp, and Gregg takes the opportunity to intrude my mouth with his tongue. He tastes like the beer he's been drinking. But there's more to his taste. The hot, wet kiss is lined with awe, love, and happiness. The cheering crowd only spurs Gregg on.

Reluctantly, I pull away, breaking our kiss.

"Yes," he says.

"Yes, what?" I ask, staring up at him, my eyes searching for the meaning behind his words.

"Yes, I'll be there. Yes, I really care. Yes, you'll never have to be alone. I love you, Macy Marie Miller."

"I love you, too," I declare, wrapping my arms around him.

The DJ interrupts us as he calls the next person on stage. Luckily for me, it's Gregg's name he calls.

"What did you do?" Gregg asks me, squinting with a questioning glare.

"Surprise," I reluctantly answer, shrugging my shoulders. With a kiss on my cheek, he reaches for my hand and pulls me to his side. With his arm wrapped around my shoulder, I nestle into his side as he picks up the microphone.

Justin Beiber's "Mistletoe" flashes on the screen.

"Really," Gregg groans.

The house lights start to dim, and I chuckle as the spotlight shines onto the stage. The music begins, and the words are highlighted on the screen. Gregg grumbles his tone-deaf rendition in the microphone, and I can't help the laugh that escapes me. I know he's hating this, but standing here, next to him, it's a classic Kodak moment.

Our friends are standing in the front row. Quinton and Brynn are dancing together. JP is dancing with a group of girls. Grant is on the dance floor, much to his dismay. The grump is wearing a scowl, but at least he's here tonight.

The night would be perfect if Chloe was here. My heart stutters, and my chest aches. I miss her so much. She should be here. We should all be together. Laughing. Dancing. Together as our little found family.

There's still a lot of tension surrounding us over the damage I've caused, but for one night, we are able to push past our differences and enjoy the moment. I have a lot of groveling to do to make up for my disappearance act and abrupt move-out. If I could take back how I handled it, I would, but life doesn't work that way. I can only hope one day I'll be able to make it up to them. One day I'll be a better friend. I pray my CTU family can look past my mistake so we can get back to our Sunday dinners and nights out together.

Turning my attention back to the stage, I watch in slow motion as the microphone drops from Gregg's hand, clambering to the ground. Feedback from the hit fills the speaker, causing the group of drunk students to wince. My eyes dart up to Gregg. But it's the sight before me that has me gasping for air as my heart plummets to the ground.

I can't breathe.

My lungs cease to exist as I fight for air.

My eyes blink as I try to wake up from this nightmare.

But it's not a nightmare.

It's reality.

I watch as Gregg's hands grip his head, his face going pale as he collapses on stage.

"Call an ambulance," I shout, diving to my knees to catch him. The music cuts off, the crowd silencing us as I watch Gregg clutch his head in between his hands.

"Gregg! Gregg!" I shout, trying to get his attention.

Reaching out, my hands rest on top of his as I cradle his head against my chest. Terrified is the only way to describe the feeling that washes over me. I'm terrified I'm losing him.

Fear grips my soul, and my stomach fights the roiling feeling to empty.

"Everything is blurry," he rasps.

This can't be happening. Please don't let it be another stroke. Bringing him here tonight was a mistake. How could I have possibly thought loud music and bright lights were a good idea?

Ten minutes later, the EMTs rush to us, pushing a gurney. I feel like I'm having an out-of-body experience as I watch my boyfriend get placed on a backboard. Brynn and the guys are at my side, but I can't hear anything they're saying.

I can't think.

I can't breathe.

I can't focus.

I just watched the love of my life get carted away, and I don't know where to go from here.

Singing in front of a crowd used to be my biggest fear. That was until this moment. This, right here, is my biggest fear. The unknown. The uncertainty. The image of him clutching his head is ingrained in my brain. I see it when I close my eyes.

And it's all my fault.

Chapter 12

It's hard to believe it's only been seventeen hours since I watched my boyfriend get carted away. Last night was a whirlwind, and I've never felt so terrified. Getting the phone call out of the blue that Gregg had a stroke was awful. But watching him collapse and clutch his head right in front of me, that was pure terror.

Never have I felt so useless.

Not to mention the guilt that flooded me. It skipped the drizzle and went straight to an immediate deluge. The onslaught of emotions nearly crushed me. Thankfully, Brynn was there to snap me out of it. Quinton drove us from The Eagles Nest to the hospital. We were seconds behind the ambulance.

I spent hours trying to reach Gregg's parents. Every text and phone call went unanswered. Eventually, I gave up trying to contact them, and I finally got ahold of Gemma's secretary, Darla. I promised Darla I would keep her updated, but the doctors assured us everything was fine, and that Gregg was just going to be kept for observation. Anger poured from me. How can parents ignore calls and texts when their son is lying in a hospital bed? I was understanding the first time. They couldn't help being out of the country. But their jobs aren't a good enough reason to ignore me and the texts that went unanswered.

Quinton and Brynn stayed in the waiting room with me until I finally kicked them out at one o'clock this morning. Sitting in a room alone gave me the perfect opportunity to reflect on how shitty of a friend I've been. No matter what the situation was, I should've had a conversation explaining why I was moving out. I should've told Chloe I understood she was scared to face her feelings with Cody and that life is short. Tomorrow is never a guarantee. But instead, I exploded on her with my fear, and she had no idea why. I don't blame her for not wanting to talk to me. I was horrible to her.

The two of us need to hash things out. I never should have taken my fear out on her, and I should have told my friends why I was moving out without a warning. The truth is, I wasn't myself, which sounds like a cop-out. But exhaustion had seeped into my bones, and fear was running through my veins. I didn't want to hear any objection to my plan of moving in with Gregg. Instead, I just kept a huge secret from the two closest people in my life.

At some point in the night, I fell asleep with my head in an awkward position until the doctor came in to inform me Gregg hadn't suffered a stroke. He just had a severe migraine that was probably triggered by the spotlight.

"Miss Miller? Miss Miller?" a voice comes from somewhere near me. Sitting up from my bent position, I tilt my head back and forth, willing the kinks to crack and disappear. I'll never miss falling asleep in a hospital waiting room chair.

Clearing my throat, I find Gregg's doctor, Dr. Grey, waiting near me. "Oh my gosh, I didn't mean to fall asleep."

A reassuring smile appears on his face. "Please don't worry at all; it's late."

He's right. I slide my phone from my pocket and glance at the screen: 3:30 a.m. We've been here for hours. "How is he?"

Dr. Grey sits in the open seat across from me. "He's fine, Miss Miller—"

"Please, call me Macy."

Dr. Grey nods. "He's fine, Macy. It appears the mixture of lights and Gregg forgetting to take his medicine caused a twinge of pain in his head. The good news is, it wasn't a stroke."

My breath catches as the words tumble from Dr. Grey's mouth. I knew the lights were a mistake, and it was my fault he went to the bar in the first place. He almost had a stroke, and it would've been my fault.

"Macy, I can see the wheels spinning. Gregg told me that you surprised him with karaoke night. But let me be clear, what happened tonight was a mixture of a lot of things. In the future, it's going to be important when going into settings with flashing lights that Gregg remembers to wear his glasses and take his medication. This is a temporary issue until his brain fully recovers. Don't beat yourself up."

Nodding, I try to let the words the doctor spoke sink in. But no matter what he says, we wouldn't have been in the hospital if I wouldn't have brought Gregg to the bar.

"Can I see him?"

Standing from his chair, he gestures for me to follow him. "Of course. We should be able to get you both out of here shortly."

"Thank you."

Falling in step behind the doctor, we walk through the beige-colored walls and shiny linoleum floors. The all-too-familiar smell of antiseptic seeps into my nose. Again, another thing I won't be missing about hospital stays. Dr. Grey stops outside of a closed door and gestures for me to enter. With a nod, I open the door and step inside.

The room is dark and quiet, the only noise coming from a machine. Gregg's lying on his back, his head tipped away from me. My feet carry me, not stopping until I'm right beside his bed. Gregg's eyes are closed, and he looks so peaceful.

I gently reach down and grip his fingers. He stirs, head turning until his eyes meet mine. Using his opposite hand, Gregg reaches for my cheek. He brushes away streams of moisture. I didn't even realize I was crying.

"Baby," Gregg rasps, emotion clogging his throat. With that word, I can't hold the sob in. My body shakes as my heart tries to catch up with my head. "Baby, I'm okay."

Letting myself relax in his touch, Gregg rubs my cheek. "I love you so much."

"I love you too, Mace. I'm sorry I forgot to take my medicine."

"I'm sorry for taking you to The Eagles Nest."

"Mace, it's not your fault. Seriously, I shouldn't have skipped my meds. I wasn't thinking about them."

"Don't do that again."

Gregg lets out a small chuckle. "I'll try not to, babe."

It was five o'clock in the morning before we stumbled into our apartment, both of us completely spent.

Today is Christmas Eve; we finally made it. I planned a quiet day of relaxing and watching football while a pot roast cooked in the oven all day. But apparently, I was wrong to assume a day at home was what we needed. When I woke up at noon, a note on my pillow was the only thing waiting for me. Not a boyfriend who spent the night in the hospital. Only a note saying Gregg had errands to run and would be gone most of the day.

Who does that?

Instead of spending the afternoon on the couch with my boyfriend, I've been lying in bed for the past hour watching Hallmark movies. My sketchpad lays next to me as I doodle a few designs. I'm hoping I'll be able to start an online store next semester where I sell the custom-made CTU shirts I make.

For the past year, I've been thrifting old school shirts and keeping them in a bin. Each year I design shirts for Brynn, Chloe, and myself to wear to football games. I love taking different designs and styles and creating unique, vintage shirts. This year for the first game, I found old shirts, cut them in half, and combined them into cute tube tops.

Every game, the girls and I get compliments on our shirts, and I decided it was time to launch an online store. The design I'm sketching today takes old denim I would cut out to form jersey numbers that would be sewn onto a shirt.

My phone vibrates on my nightstand, causing me to jump out of my skin. It's been so quiet with just the TV playing in a soft volume. Picking up the phone, I see *Mom* flash across the screen. My shoulders slump in disappointment. It's not that I don't want to talk to my mom. I was just hoping to finally hear from Gregg.

"Hey, Mom," I rasp out, clearing my throat from not using it yet today.

"Oh, sweetie, you sound exhausted," she starts, concern lacing her voice. "How's Gregg?"

Moisture immediately gathers in my eyes, and I feel the slightest quiver of my chin. The Christmas movie and sketches were doing a decent job of keeping the thoughts at bay, but there's nothing like a call from your mom to bring all the emotions to the surface.

"Mom," I gasp out as the dam breaks. Tears stream down my face as I fight to keep the sob from exploding.

"Macy Marie. Sweetie. Hey, take a deep breath."

I do as she says and focus on inhaling a deep breath. I hold it in my lungs for a couple seconds before slowly letting the air slip past my lips.

"It's all my fault, Mom," I admit, still trying to calm my breathing. "He left this morning before I woke up."

"What do you mean?"

"He left me a note saying he had errands to run. He should be home resting. Why would he just disappear with a note saying he'd be gone until evening? Do you think he blames me for taking him there last night? I mean, I understand if he blames me. Hell, I am blaming myself. I knew better. Deep down, I knew he shouldn't have been there, but I wasn't thinking. I just wanted to have some fun. I screwed up."

"Oh baby girl, there's nothing wrong with that. Seriously, sweetie. You can't blame yourself," she responds. "He admitted he forgot to take his medicine. You both forgot his glasses. At the end of the day, it was an accident, and accidents happen."

I hum at her words. While they may be true, it still doesn't help alleviate the guilt. The few texts he's sent me have all been one-word responses, which are the freaking worst. But at least he's answering me and hasn't collapsed somewhere.

"I mean it, Macy. It was an *accident*. Accidents are going to happen. It's how you work past those incidents that will determine how your relationship will flourish. That boy loves you. I've known it for weeks now. You two might have been fooling yourselves, but I saw it every time I FaceTimed you."

"What do you mean?" Pushing my sketchpad out of the way, I sit up higher on the bed.

"I mean, what college guy would agree to let some girl move in with him if he didn't have feelings for her? College boys are idiots and only think about one thing. Your brothers might've thought they were being sneaky, but I knew about the girls they were always chasing. Guys only think about whatever their interest is and sex. It's human nature. But Gregg wanted you living with him. He could've objected. He could've moved home. But he didn't, Mace. He chose you."

"Mom, I'm scared."

"Love is scary, my sweet girl. Love is putting your faith in someone else. It's choosing to be selfless when you want to be selfish. It's choosing to confide in someone else. It's about being vulnerable, patient, kind, and fighting for your futures. Don't take each other for granted. Fight for your love, and it will be the best accomplishment of your life. Your dad and I have been fighting for our love for thirty-seven years. It hasn't been easy; that's for damn sure."

I chuckle at her admission. I've always admired their love. My parents work hard, and they always show each other how much they mean to one another. It's the kind of love I grew up craving. I knew by watching them, I'd never settle for anyone who didn't appreciate me.

"Thanks, Mom."

"Of course, sweetheart. Now, when that Gregg gets his ass home, give him the benefit of the doubt. Maybe he was scared and just needed to do some reflecting on his own. Remember, it's Christmas Eve; a miracle was about to be born. Remind him of what he has at home, and show him what he means to you. I love you, Macy Marie."

"I love you too, Mom. Thanks for checking on me."

"Of course, baby girl. Merry Christmas Eve."

After hanging up the phone, I can't help but feel lighter. My mom always knows when I need to hear from her. But I guess that's what happens when you're best friends and talk to each other a hundred times a day.

And with her comment of reminding him what he means to me, the perfect idea hops into my head. Tossing the covers off of me, I hurry out of our shared bedroom and head to the guest room, which used to be mine. The guest bedroom has been converted back into a guest space, with the exception of my vanity, since we arrived back from Michigan. I like having my own space to do my hair and makeup without taking away space in the master bedroom.

I head straight to the closet, where I have a bin of new purchases waiting to be worn. I'm forever grateful for my organized closet. I don't know how people handle not knowing where they put things.

Finding the red ensemble, I grab it and head to the bathroom for a full girl shower—shave, exfoliate, moisturize, the works. Turning the shower handle, I slide my phone from my pocket, and I start queuing up a playlist on Spotify while I wait for the water to warm up.

"Mace!" Gregg calls out, and I hear the front door close. I've spent the last hour and a half primping for Gregg's return. I transformed myself from a bed monster who was still in her pajamas to a whole new version of myself. Before slipping into the red ensemble I grabbed from the closet, I prepped the apartment to set the mood for the night. The living room is cascaded in a soft, sexy glow from the lit fireplace, and the Christmas lights are turned on.

After the main space was done, I focused on getting the bedroom ready. Now, a bottle of champagne is chilling in an ice bucket, and white LED candles are peppered throughout the room, illuminating the bed, all while a sexy playlist croons through the speakers. I've been hiding out here ever since, waiting for Gregg's return.

Finally, I hear his footsteps fill the hallway through the cracked bedroom door. I made sure to leave my door wide open with the lights off so he knew I wasn't in there. Sitting up straighter, I watch as the door slowly opens.

"Mace you in—" Gregg's words freeze as he stops in his tracks. His eyes widen as he takes me in. Sitting on my knees on top of the covers, I'm waiting for him as he walks through the door with nothing but a red satin thong covering my lower half and a matching strapless bra that ties in an oversized, red satin bow, exposing my fair, toned skin. My hair is down in voluminous curls with my makeup done subtly.

I've never felt more vulnerable than I do right now, sitting half-naked in front of the man I've given my whole heart to. He's also the man who ghosted me for the day, and I don't know what that means for us.

Sorry, Mom, I don't think this is what you had in mind for showing him what he was missing.

Gregg still hasn't moved from the doorway, and if it wasn't for the heat in his gaze that is searing my skin, I would be curling in on myself with embarrassment. My tongue slips free, running across my bottom lip, causing Gregg to follow the trail. Wetness is pooling between my thighs, and the urge to touch myself grows.

"Do it," Gregg rasps out as if he can read my mind. "You want to touch yourself, don't you?"

"Maybe." A sultry smirk finds itself on my face as I tilt my head. Slowly, I bring my hand in between my breasts, skating my fingers along my breastbone, down my stomach, and settling them on the satin string of my thong. Wiggling the thin piece of fabric up and down, I tease Gregg and watch his eyes darken with desire.

In two large strides, he's standing right in front of me, gazing down at my half-dressed body.

"Hey, beautiful," he greets, caressing the outside of my thighs in soft, gentle strokes.

My body is thrumming under his touch. My pussy flutters as wetness coats the inside of my thighs. Tilting my head up, my lips find him in a soft touch.

"Hey, handsome," I respond in a whisper against his mouth.

"Is this the heart-felt present you picked out for me?" A grin spreads across his face.

"Nope," I answer, pressing another kiss on his lips before pulling back. "This is to show you what you've been missing all day. I missed you."

"Shit, I missed you, too." His hand flies behind my neck, gripping me in a powerful hold and forcing my head to meet his lips in a searing, toe-curling kiss. His touch is laced with a mixture of an apology for leaving me and heat and desire.

I'm reaching for the hem of his shirt—desperate to get him as exposed as I feel. Ripping his shirt above his head, I toss it to the side. My fingers graze his warm skin as goosebumps pebble across his chest. With a flick to his nipple, I chuckle against his mouth as his body shudders away from my touch. I know he doesn't like that.

"You brat," he murmurs against my lips. He trails kisses from my lips—nipping and sucking— down my neck before he presses me backward. My back lands against our sheets as my hand moves between us. Gripping and tugging, my fingers work to loosen his belt to free him from his jeans.

Taking the hint, Gregg moves from on top of me, quickly discarding his jeans and boxer briefs before climbing back on top and settling between my legs. My body comes alive under his touch. My pussy is needy as she weeps for more. Gregg's hands graze my skin, causing goosebumps to erupt and my already pebbled nipples to peak even harder. Trailing open mouth kisses down my body, his hands catch on the thin strap of my thong. With one swift move, he's ripping them from my body. I gasp as the elastic breaks. But before I can react, Gregg's lips are soothing the spot where the material broke. His tongue finds my dripping center in one sweep.

"This pussy," he hums in appreciation. "Always so sweet and ready for me."

I'm a needy mess for him. "Gregg!"

He slides up my body, sucking a nipple in his mouth, causing my back to bow off the bed, desperate for me. With a pop, he lets go, and his mouth finds mine. His thick cock is lined up perfectly with my weeping center.

In one swift motion, Gregg thrusts inside of me. I cry out as the pain from him stretching me mixes with the pleasure of our bodies coming together. He slides out of me, his eyes remaining locked on mine, as he thrusts inside again. Desperate to feel him deeper, I push his shoulder, encouraging us to switch positions. With one quick move, I'm straddling Gregg's naked body.

"Damn, Mace," Gregg groans as I grind down on him. Leaning forward, I watch as he slides almost completely out of me. Squatting back down, we both groan in appreciation as my body swallows him in one quick thrust.

My hips begin rocking.

Twisting and rotating.

Taking him deeper and deeper.

Gregg's hands find my breasts as he roughly massages them. Slipping his hand under my red bow, his fingers drag over my sensitive peaks. With a twist, he uses my nipples to pull me toward him, causing my body to fall on top of him, his lips catching me. My hips continue rotating as Gregg meets me, thrust for thrust as our tongues melt into each other. A sharp pinch against my erect nipple has me screaming as the pending orgasm builds.

"Oh, God," I yell. "I'm so close."

Angling my hips, I grind down against him, working my needy clit against his pubic bone. The friction causes my orgasm to explode from my body.

I cry out, and in the next moment, I find myself on my back again as Gregg leans above me, fisting his cock until his release is coating my stomach.

"Merry Christmas Eve," I rasp out as he collapses next to me. Our chests heave as our limbs remain tangled together. The two of us are too spent to ask questions about where he's been all day. That's a conversation for another day.

Chapter 13

Soft, gentle kisses trail down my exposed spine, slowly bringing me out of my peaceful sleep. My body begins to stir.

"Merry Christmas, beautiful," Gregg whispers into my ear.

I hum. "Merry Christmas," I say, rolling over beneath him. Only the soft material of the sheet separates us. "Ready to go open some presents?"

"I've got the only gift I need right here." Bending down, he places a sweet kiss on my lips. "Morning breath and all."

"Oh gosh," I gasp, turning my face away from him, embarrassment coating my cheeks. He chuckles as he slides off of me and out of our warm bed. The sheet falls as he walks away, exposing his naked body. I admire the rippled muscles that lead down to the round globes of his ass.

"Would you stop staring at my ass?" he muses, ruffling through his closet. Grinning, I watch him dig through his mess. For a golfer, Gregg stays in incredible shape. Before the stroke, he would spend a few days a week working out at the campus gym.

I cringe watching him dig through his chaos. Now that we are sharing the same room, it's time for Gregg to get a reality check and learn how to organize his closet.

"Here," he says, tossing me a shopping bag. "I picked these up for us the day we went to the mall."

My brow quirks as I rifle through the tissue paper. Pulling out the contents, I admire the soft, red tartan plaid pajama sleep shirt. Glancing up, I see that Gregg has already slipped on a pair of matching plaid sleep pants and a green cotton t-shirt.

"Gregg, this was so sweet."

"It wasn't a big deal. I saw them, and then I felt the material and knew we needed to have them," he says with a shrug.

Slipping the shirt over my head, I'm grateful the dress is loose enough that it doesn't need to be buttoned each and every time I take it on and off. I slide out of bed and rush to the bathroom to rid myself of monster breath. Gregg sidles up beside me, and the two of us run through our morning routines. I stare at our reflections in the mirror and smile around the foaming toothpaste.

Is this what domesticated bliss feels like? If so, sign me up forever.

"Wait," Gregg yells, jumping up from his spot next to the tree. I'm too stunned to say anything, too busy admiring that he didn't wince or limp at the sudden change in movement. Shaking my head, I watch as Gregg swings open the door, heading into the hallway in his pajamas, sans shoes.

"Gregg!" I shout after him, but it's too late. The door shuts before he has a chance to hear me.

Shaking my head at his sudden change in demeanor, a happy feeling rushes over me, and I think about how perfect our morning has been.

The sweet, nutty smell of coffee cake baking in the oven surrounds us while Ralphie and the *A Christmas Story* gang are playing softly in the background. At some point this morning, Gregg must've snuck out to make coffee for us. I had a holiday-themed mug filled with peppermint-flavored goodness.

Our tree was overflowing with presents since our families shipped our gifts here after Gregg and I decided to celebrate Christmas just the two of us. Surprisingly, my parents didn't put up a fight. I think it helped that Gregg and I were home last week, and it didn't make sense to fly back. In no time, we had opened the gifts and littered wrapping paper all around our living room. No wonder my dad was always close by with a trash bag whenever gifts were involved. It was a gift wrap explosion in our living room.

After we unwrapped presents from others, Gregg and I exchanged ours. I watched with reluctance as Gregg opened his gift from me. Anxiety had me feeling like I might've been a little too presumptuous with his. But his face widened in a bright smile when I watched him unwrap his new putter and a new box of golf balls.

There's no doubt in my mind Gregg will be back on the green in no time. His recovery is going exceptionally well, and I've noticed a change in his grip recently.

The last few weeks also inspired me to give him a bucket list journal. We've done so many first activities together this month, and documenting them in a special journal just felt right. Inside the pages were photos from the Christmas lights, photos that Miles took of Gregg seeing snow for the first time, and fun candids I took without Gregg knowing. I can't wait to continue filling the journal together as we make more memories.

A few minutes pass, and I'm starting to wonder if he's okay. Maybe that jump bothered his leg, and he's having trouble walking, but then the front door flies open, easing my anxiety. From my position on the floor next to the tree, I can only see him from the chest up, the couch blocking the rest of him.

"Close your eyes," he says, shutting the door behind him.

"Where did you go?" I ask while closing my eyes like I was asked to do.

Noises come from the back of the couch and get closer. The sound of metal clinging together fills the air, and my anxiety starts to heighten. I hate surprises and not being able to see what's around me.

"Open," he says.

Blinking my eyes one, twice, three times, I find Gregg sitting next to me, holding a ball of fur in his hands. With a small nudge, I watch as the ball of fur begins to move. A head peeks up from Gregg's arms, and I let out a gasp.

"Gregg!" I exclaim, reaching out to grab the chestnut and white-colored puppy from his arms. "Oh my gosh, look at this sweetheart." Bringing the cutie up to my chest, I cuddle the puppy into my neck.

"I thought we could name him Boone after the stuffed animal you used to carry around when you were little."

My eyes snap from the sweet, little puppy in my arms to my amazing boyfriend. "How did you know about Boone?"

He laughs. "You have Max to thank for that. He's been texting me pictures of you and your stuffed animal. He told me all about him while we were in Michigan. He even went as far as suggesting a Cavalier King Charles Spaniel as the perfect gift for you. It seems my girlfriend has a soft spot for animals."

Flinging my body, I protect the puppy and wrap my free arm around Gregg's neck. I climb into his lap—Boone between us—as my lips find his. "Thank you so much. This is the best gift."

"It's the least I could do, Macy. You've given me so much, so much that I could never thank you enough, but I thought Boone was a good start."

"He's perfect," I say, looking down at the angel baby in my arms. "His little red sweater is just too cute. Where was he?"

"So remember that errand I had to run yesterday? Well, I went to Fort Worth with Rick to pick him up. Turns out Rick knew a family that had puppies."

"What? You did a five-hour round trip to pick him up yesterday? After you were in the hospital all night? I thought you were second-guessing things between us." As much as I love this cute little puppy, Gregg should not have been in the car for that long.

"Macy, I would never. You're stuck with me," Gregg leans in and kisses my temple. "And don't worry; Rick drove the whole time."

"Okay, but where was he last night?" Boone nudged my palm, waiting for me to start petting him again. My fingers glide through his soft fur.

"And we have Linda down the hall to thank for watching him for us. It turns out she has a real soft spot for puppies, and you. When I told her my idea, she all but begged for me to let her keep Boone company last night."

"That Linda." Linda is our friendly, middle-aged neighbor who lives at the end of our floor. She's turned into almost a mother hen to Gregg and I, always checking in on us when she sees us in the hall. Since Gregg had his stroke, she makes sure to drop off a meal to us once a week, even though we insist she doesn't need to.

Gregg reaches down and begins scratching behind Boone's ears. He must love it because Boone licks Gregg's fingers. "She also volunteered to watch him or let him out whenever we need help."

"I never want to let this cutie out of my sight," I say to Boone as I nuzzle my face into his coat.

"I never want to let *this* cutie out of my sight," he repeats, but he isn't looking at Boone; he's staring at me.

Leaning in, I give Gregg another kiss. It seems Boone wants in on the action, too, as we feel a scratchy, wet tongue lick across our chins. Both of us separate, our foreheads resting together, as we look down at those big, brown eyes.

"I have a feeling we won't be telling him no," I say with a chuckle.

"Great, that's another one I won't ever be able to say no to."

Reaching behind me, I move my hand around until my fingers touch the cold metal of my phone. Bringing it in front of me, I swipe over, waiting for the camera to load. Positioning the screen in front of us, I look over to Gregg.

"Let's take our first family picture!" Excitement laces my words. I'm still in shock that this is my life. I can't believe my brother told Gregg about my stuffed animal. I didn't think Max would be the one to encourage us to get a puppy together.

Gregg reaches over and takes the phone from my hand while he wraps his other arm around me. The two of us get into a comfortable pose and adjust Boone until he's clearly seen in the square box on the screen. I watch as Gregg's eyes find mine through the lens, and my smile doubles. With a quick click, Gregg takes our photo before handing the phone back to me.

Leaning up, I plant my mouth to his. Not wanting the moment to end, but knowing my parents are probably waiting for me to wish them a Merry Christmas, I thumb out a Christmas greeting and attach our photo. Pressing send, I wait for the replies to start filtering through.

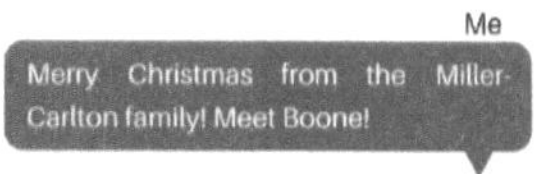

Gregg and I read as the replies come in rapid succession. The Millers should be getting ready to sit down and have brunch in the lodge before opening gifts together. It's weird not being able to be with my family this year. It's the first Christmas I've missed in twenty-one years. But before I have a chance to dwell on missing my family, Gregg's phone is ringing.

Reaching over, I watch him read the screen with confusion creasing his forehead. "My mom is FaceTiming us."

"Well, answer it," I practically shout, nudging him to accept the incoming call.

He swipes the video open, and Gemma fills the screen. She's sitting in front of windows that overlook downtown Dallas—the backdrop to her office.

"Merry Christmas!" she shouts excitedly before we have a chance to greet her.

"Merry Christmas," Gregg and I repeat in unison before Gregg continues. "Mom, meet Boone." He holds the camera down until the sweet furry face fills the screen.

"Aw, he is just precious!" She takes the next few minutes talking to Boone. Gregg finds my gaze, and my face spreads into a wide grin.

"I'm the worst," Gemma starts, interrupting Gregg and I's connection. "Part of your Christmas gift wasn't going to get to you both in time. I didn't want to risk it getting to you late, so instead, I just emailed it to you both."

Immediately, I grab my phone and scroll through my apps until the white envelope appears. Opening the app, the first email waiting for me is from Gemma. Clicking the message, I gasp as I read the words on the screen.

"Gemma," I rasp, covering my open mouth with my palm.

Gregg peers over my shoulder before finding his mom's eyes. "Two tickets to the Bahamas?"

"Surprise!" Gemma's wide smile fills the screen. "I thought the four of us could celebrate New Years together. I'd love to keep getting to know you, Macy, and I miss spending time with my son."

"Thank you," I say to Gemma.

"Of course, sweetie. Merry Christmas, you two. I love you."

"Love you, too, Mom." The words leave Gregg's mouth, and I can hear the lump forming in his throat.

And with that, my heart is overflowing with love and happiness.

This is the year of the Christmas scramble, where everything we thought we knew or thought would happen completely changed course. I should be in Michigan with my family, but as I'm sitting here in this apartment, I'm right where I'm supposed to be.

I've never felt more at home in all my life.

Life has a way of disturbing your plans, of making you question what your future looks like. But the holiday spirit has a way of showing you that you don't need a plan. All you need is a little bit of belief, a sprinkle of courage, and a whole lot of love.

THE END

Author's Note

I would like to take this opportunity to thank my sister-in-law, Brittany, for letting me share her story in my book. Gregg's stroke and medical history came directly from my sister-in-law's own experience.

In her mid-twenties and after having three small children, Brittany suffered a stroke after battling massive, debilitating migraines every month since the 8th grade. After being treated for the stroke, the doctors determined that the cause was a small hole in her heart that never closed during development. Once repaired, Brittany has been able to live a migraine free life.

I understand that not every person who suffers from migraines will have the same experience. This is just one story. My hope is that you prioritize your health. Living with debilitating migraines is not normal. Always take care of yourselves, friends.

Acknowledgements

Surprise! This Christmas novella was so much fun to write. I'm honestly shocked I was able to give you Gregg and Macy's story so quickly, but here we are. I hope you loved seeing more of what happened behind the scenes with Gregg and Macy from the glimpses in The Late Hit.

To my husband, I love you. Thank you for always encouraging me to keep on writing. When I came to you with this idea, you were all for it. I love that you are my biggest fan. I wouldn't want anyone else in my corner hyping me up and talking me down when imposter syndrome gets the best of me.

To my kids, thank you both for being so excited to see *Mommy's book*. You both are so sweet with your excitement towards my writing. I love you two so much.

To my sister-in-law, Brittany - Thank you for letting me share your story with my readers. Gregg's story comes straight from the pages of my sister-in-law's book. Britt, thank you for giving me your story, for helping with the medical jargon, and for being an early reader to make sure that I told your story correctly.

To my parents - Growing up, you always made sure Natalie and I would have a memorable Christmas season. Thank you for always making each year magical. The memories made growing up will last a lifetime and I'm so excited to share our traditions with my kids. Also, thank you for showing us what real love looks like.

To my sister, Natalie- I don't know what I would do without you. Thank you for always checking my captions for spelling and grammar issues, for letting me bounce ideas off you, for helping out with the kids when I need to hit a deadline, and for always being my cheerleader.

To Amy Tackett- Girl, where would I be without you?! Thank you for listening to my endless voice memos as I give you random brain dumps for all of my story ideas. Thank you for always talking me off the ledge and for cheering me on throughout this journey. I'm so glad to have you in my life. Thank you for editing and proofreading. This book would be a hot mess without your help.

To Melissa, my incredible cover designer at Mel D Designs- Mel, I can't even begin to thank you enough for whipping out this cover in a DAY. I absolutely love how you brought my vision to life. You made me feel seen and I appreciate you more than words... ha, and I'm supposed to be a writer. I'm so excited to continue our journey for the rest of the series.

To my incredible Alpha & Beta Team: Allie, Brianna, Chelsea, Christina, Katlyn, Taylor, and Terri- You ladies are the best! The time you all spent reading, analyzing, and collecting feedback to make this novella stronger doesn't go unnoticed. I wouldn't be here today if it wasn't for your help in fixing plot holes, honing in the character development, and making sure the story lined up with the timeline from The Late Hit. Thank you!

To my ARC & Street Team- Your endless support means the absolute world. Thank you so much for every like, comment, and share in getting the word out about this novella. I am overwhelmed by your constant support. I appreciate you all for being on this journey with me.

Lastly, to you the reader- Thank you for picking up The Christmas Scramble! I hope my words were able to bring you a little bit of Christmas cheer this holiday season.

Not ready to leave Central Texas University?

Have you read book one in the CTU Eagles series? If you want banter, plenty of sexual tension, feeling all the feels, and a twist you don't see coming, check out Brynn and Quinton's story.

Keep reading for a sneak peek of the first chapter of The Late Hit.

Want to see a bonus chapter from Gregg's point of view? Head to my website: authoralexisbuxton.com and sign up for my newsletter. A bonus chapter will be sent to you by December 25th.

Click here to sign up

https://optimistic-cake-89826.myflodesk.com/lq9goai3y

Want to watch sparks fly between CTU's playboy base-ball pitcher and the quiet, sweet bookworm? Check out *The Change Up*, an enemies-to-lovers, second-chance romance releasing Spring 2024!

Preorder now and add on Goodreads!

https://mybook.to/wv1aM

Chapter One: Brynn

I'm never drinking again.

The soft chirp of birds fills the silence around me as the sky is slowly starting to wake. Steadily, I begin to rise from bed, only to be met with the pounding in my head that is trying to consume me.

Another morning, another hangover.

Glancing around the room, I search for my clothes. There is no way I am making the trek to my car in only a borrowed Central Texas Eagles football shirt that looks more like a dress than a shirt on me.

I throw the covers off me, sitting up slowly, trying to avoid the inevitable feeling of the room spinning and the need to empty my stomach.

"The sun isn't even out," Quinton groans from the makeshift bed on the floor.

"I've got class," I reply, jumping out of his warm bed. It's either I get up now, or I'll cave in and spend all morning lying in bed.

"Besides, don't you have to get up soon for weightlifting?"

"Coach pushed weightlifting back until eight o'clock, thank god," Quinton replies.

"Lucky you," I say. "Meet me at the Student Union at eleven thirty for lunch?"

"Yeah, see you later," Q says, rolling over and bringing his blanket up to his chin. He looks so comfortable. I wish I could say the same about myself. Why did I want the best professor for my Psychology 3600 class? And why does he only teach eight a.m. classes?

Locating my clothes on his desk chair, I throw off Quinton's T-shirt, toss it in the pile of clothes that I assume are dirty, and pull on my clothes from last night. I'm always thankful when parties are casual and not themed. It makes the next morning less awkward. Cutoff jean shorts, a cute tank, and Converse don't scream "walk of shame" quite like a tight dress and heels.

Stumbling over to the nightstand, I pick up my round, tortoise-framed glasses and pop in a piece of gum. Gum will have to do until I make it back to my town house to freshen up. The inside of my mouth feels like I licked the mat that holds overflow draft beer at bars. *Gross!*

Stepping out of Quinton's bedroom, I notice that the house is calm and quiet, the total opposite of last night. But before I can take in my surroundings, I am met with the stench of weed, sticky floors, and littered beer cans.

God—this house is a disaster.

Dubbed the Football House around campus, Quinton's house is a three-story brick colonial. His parents purchased the house for his older brother to live in while he was in college. Once Damien graduated, Quinton moved in with some of his teammates and younger brother. The Football House is the place to party on campus. They're known for throwing the wildest parties. But since a lot is riding on the line for all the guys that live here, the parties are usually invite-only to keep the crowd under some control.

Since I don't live nearby, Q lets me crash in his room after parties, as long as he isn't hooking up with some chick. On the nights he's got a lady, I crash in the third-story movie room. The couch isn't as comfortable as Q's bed, but it gets the job done. And it definitely gets the job done. It's the most comfortable bed I've ever slept on. It's like lying on a cloud. There's no way I'd give up sleeping in this bed if it was mine. But Quinton does every time I stay over. He never sleeps in the bed with me, he always takes the floor.

Quinton Boyd is not only a Power Five running back for the CTU Eagles, but he's a potential first-round draft pick in the NFL. With Q's stats, it's a no-brainer that he will go first round, top ten. He's insanely talented, can bench and squat an ungodly amount, and makes defenders look stupid. While he may have the NFL's eye, he also has the campus eating out of the palm of his hand. The guys want to be him, the ladies want under him, and I'm lucky enough to call him my best friend.

Football season kicks off next weekend. Every September, the team kicks off the season and the new school year with their weekly Thirsty Thursday party. The guys always say their Thirsty Thursday nights are going to be low-key, but the parties are far from laid-back. Last night's party got a little carried away.

That's what happens when people start talking about a party, especially one at the Football House.

Carefully, I make my way down the old, hardwood staircase, stepping over a few bodies of passed-out partygoers, and walk straight into the kitchen. For some reason, during the party, I ended up taking my Converse off, and now I have no idea where they are. This brings me to a better question than where, but why would taking my shoes off in *this house* even cross my mind?

Pulling a kitchen chair to the refrigerator, I stand and look to see if someone put them on top. Nope, not there. Glancing around the open concept kitchen, dining room, and living room, I see a lot of random things, but no Converse. My eyes keep scanning and snag on something hanging from the patio. Stepping off the chair, I make my way to the kitchen window and peer out over the yard. And there they are. My shoes are dangling from the patio roof. There's no way I'm going out to get them now. Deciding to let them hang, I make my way to the front door barefoot.

It's six o'clock in the morning, my head is pounding, and I got four hours of sleep, but I can't help but take in the quiet campus. I don't think there's anything better than the morning on campus. Even hungover, I can truly appreciate the historic campus that makes up Central Texas University, a one-hundred-fifty-year-old university. The school hasn't lost any of its charm over the years and somehow, like a fine wine, keeps getting better with age.

The mature trees line the sidewalks and are flourishing. Instead of paved streets, CTU features a majority of brick-lined streets. The buildings that make up the campus are all original with stunning architectural designs.

Attending CTU had always been my brother's and my dream. I'm so glad I decided to attend, even though his plans changed. Thankfully, I met Quinton. He helped ease the guilt of being at CTU.

Quinton and I met freshman year. But we weren't instant friends.

The first week of school was 'icebreaker' week. Each day, we were assigned mandatory activities. Quinton and I were assigned a lot of the same activities. My team kept beating Q's team, and apparently, he's a sore loser.

Then at the end of the week, we were both at the same party. Q and I were paired opposites in a beer pong game. He and his partner were on their ninth game-winning streak, when my partner and I beat them. We continued our winning streak and won the little tournament that was going on.

My cockiness might've shone through as I ran my mouth to all of his friends about how much he sucked. I might have been a little—okay, a lot—drunk.

Karma would then come around and bite me in the ass when we both had the same mandatory freshman class. The only open seat was beside Quinton, which made us partners for the semester. It ended up being a blessing because we quickly became best friends and have been inseparable since.

Making the ten-minute drive to my town house, I park in my designated spot. I share a three-bedroom house with my two best friends, Chloe and Macy. Before I get a chance to open the front door, I'm forced to halt my entrance as Macy opens it with a tall man behind her. He looks familiar, but I can't quite place where I recognize him from. Story of my life.

"Well, looks like it's a good morning for you," I greet Macy and her friend.

Her face flushes red as she lets her friend out the front door.

"Gregg, this is my roommate Brynn Wilder. Brynn, this is Gregg Carlton." She introduces us as Gregg reaches his hand out for me to shake. "Thanks for last night, Gregg," Macy says, turning her attention back to him.

Gregg leans down and kisses Macy on her cheek, her face turning even redder.

"See you around, Macy."

He turns and walks down the three steps off our front porch and heads down the sidewalk toward the guest parking.

Shutting the door after I walk inside, Macy turns to me.

"I could say the same about you," Macy retorts.

"Oh please, you know I stayed with Quinton," I reply, placing my keys on the hook by the front door before heading into our kitchen.

As put together as I try to be, if I don't put my keys on the hook right away, I'll be tearing the house apart trying to find them. Once I put them in the freezer, and it took four hours to find them.

Macy is right on my heels, and we both make our way to the Keurig. Coffee is essential this morning. Caffeine is vital every morning, but especially today. I will never understand people who don't drink coffee. That first sip of hot coffee rolls through my veins and warms up my black heart. It's the absolute best.

Reaching up in the cabinet above our coffee cart, I pull down two mugs. One is a yellow mug that says *"My anxiety is chronic, but this ass is iconic"* and the other is a blush-colored mug with *"Have fun. Don't do stupid shit. Study hard. Go to class, Call Home"* written on it. The mug is definitely not from my collection. While I'm grabbing the mugs, Macy is loading the Keurig with Death Wish coffee. Turning to me, she grabs a mug from my outstretched hand, places it under the drip, and resumes our conversation.

"When are you two going to give in to all of that sexual chemistry? I see it. Chloe sees it. Cody sees it. Everyone sees it but you two," she says, leaning against the counter.

A sigh escapes my mouth as my eyes roll in a dramatic fashion. Grabbing my mug from under the Keurig, I take my first sip.

Ahh that first taste is like the perfect hit.

I can feel my soul waking up, putting Bitch Brynn to rest.

"Mace, I'm going to stop you right there. I'm too hungover to have this conversation with you for the hundredth time. Q is my friend. That's it. End of," I say, turning to head out of the kitchen. Before I make it all the way out of the room, I turn over my shoulder and say, "I've got to shower and head to class."

Macy just stands there, leaning against the counter with a smirk on her face.

Quinton and I are constantly getting asked why we aren't together. Even in college, people can't understand our relationship. He's my best friend.

Do I find him attractive? Of course. I have eyes and a pulse. He's stunning, there's no denying that.

Quinton Boyd has flawless, medium-brown skin marked with black ink. Tattoos line his left arm from his shoulder to his wrist. Across his strong chest is a giant eagle with its wings spread open, stretching from one pectoral muscle to the other. Inked down his rib cage on his right side is a detailed cross. His black hair is kept in a tight fade on the sides, with longer curls on top. A gold chain always lays around his neck with a small cross at the center—it was a gift from his grandma Cleo.

And his smile. Goddamn, Quinton Boyd has a panty-dropping smile, perfectly straight, white teeth and the tiniest dimple on his lower cheek, but only on the left side. The dreamiest brown eyes that remind me of rich dark coffee are outlined with an umber-brown ring.

But what makes him most attractive is his personality. He's cocky, yet charming and protective, with a wild side. He's a man of few words. The quiet one who sits back and listens. Quinton would give the shirt off his back for a stranger, and he's the first person to help an old lady cross the road. Believe me, I've seen him do it many times.

But the thing is, I value our friendship too much to ever even think about crossing that line.

And I'm too damaged to be in a relationship, especially with someone as good as Quinton.

The next hour flies by as I shower and get ready for Friday classes. It's the end of the first week, and I only have two classes. I throw on a black pair of bike shorts and an oversized graphic T-shirt with a pair of dad-style tennis shoes. Since I don't have time to fix my hair or makeup, I settle for tossing my blonde hair in a claw clip. I am forever thankful to whoever decided to bring back claw clips—y'all are the real MVPs.

Quickly, I apply a small layer of mascara. It's the only makeup I have time for. Before I leave my room, I put on my gold bar necklace that has the letter 'B' engraved on it. This necklace is my favorite possession, and it only comes off when I shower. I try to never leave the house without it.

Running down the stairs, I stop at the entry closet and pull out my backpack and grab my keys off the hook. Sitting on our entryway table is a cup of on-the-go oatmeal and a note.

B,

Didn't mean to upset you this morning. Have a kick ass Friday.

XO,

M

PS- Say this out loud and put that shit in the universe. "I am worthy of an amazing life"

Macy is all about manifesting. She says things are more likely to come true if we speak it out loud to the universe.

Taking a deep breath in and exhaling slowly, I close my eyes and look up to the ceiling before repeating: "I am worthy of an amazing life."

And with that, I rush outside to my car.

Finding a parking spot on campus after nine a.m. is a challenge, but before nine a.m. is a piece of cake. There's a spot two rows in and five cars in. Doing one more glance at my appearance in the rearview mirror, I decide it's as good as it's going to get. Thankfully, my glasses help hide some of the dark circles under my eyes. Why did I sign up for such an early class? Oh yeah, hot Prof. Peters. Grabbing my bag, I exit my car, locking it as I head toward all of the walking zombies, I mean students, who are looking as tired and hungover as I am.

I enter Rogers Hall, finding the elevator and stepping on with others. Pushing through the bodies and standing shoulder-to-shoulder until the doors open on the third floor. I follow the rushing crowd to Lecture Hall 302, one of the largest lecture halls on campus. It's a three-story auditorium and holds a couple hundred students.

Descending the steps, I walk toward the middle of the room. Glancing around, I finally spot a familiar person and head toward him. He must hear me coming, because Cody glances up with a questioning look before a smile takes over his face.

"Yo, B, I'm glad to see someone I know in this class," Cody says as he shuffles his backpack out of my way.

Cody Jacobs is a pitcher on the baseball team, and the two of us run in similar crowds. Like Quinton, Cody is one of my best friends. No, I'm not a jersey chaser, I just prefer hanging out with the jocks. Plopping down in the seat next to him, I fold my arms on the desk and rest my head on my arms. There are about ten minutes before class begins and I'm planning on taking full advantage of the calm.

"Ohemgee, Cody, why does Peters have to teach the Friday morning lecture?" I whine.

"What's the matter, B? A little hungover?" Cody asks with a chuckle as he spins his pen on his fingers.

I don't even bother with an answer, just look at him with my eyes squinting.

He lets out a chuckle. "Let me guess, you're taking tonight off?"

"I'm hungover, not dead," I answer. "I think we are heading to The Eagles' Nest for happy hour and wings."

"Dude, I'm in. The Eagles' Nest has the best wings around."

The Eagles' Nest, yes the bar is named after the CTU Eagles, is a local campus essential. While the Football House is the place to party on campus, The Eagles' Nest is the spot to be when you need to unwind off campus. They serve cheap food and cheap beer. There's always some kind of local band on Friday nights. It's the place to be around campus. The owner loves football, and Q can usually get a few tables reserved for us.

"I'll have Q add you for the total," I say, finally pulling my head off my arms and reaching into my backpack to pull out my iPad and stylus.

"So, B, you and Q?" Cody begins before I cut him off.

"Don't even think about finishing that question, Cody."

"Just making sure nothing has changed," Cody replies with a smirk.

I shake my head. Cody has been trying to get me to go out with him for a while, and for some reason, I just can't bring myself to say yes. Cody is a good guy, the best guy, and he'd be a good time—at least, that's the rumor on campus—but that's all it would be, a good time. And I prefer not to mess around with close friends. It always makes everything awkward, and then all of our friends are in our business. I'm all about that "no strings attached hook-up."

Before we have a chance to finish our conversation, the first-floor door opens, and Professor Peters walks in and slams the door. Peters is a second-year professor and he's not much older than we are. He is hot, hot, hot. As in, model hot. He's like that guy on Instagram you stumble upon and immediately become obsessed with. Tall, lean-built, but not skinny, more like a swimmer's build. He has dark hair, dark-green eyes, and a golden tan. Not to mention a permanent five o'clock shadow that he keeps groomed to always look a little disheveled.

"Good morning, this is Psych 3600," Professor Peters greets the class. His eyes look around the lecture hall. "If you're not a psych major, you shouldn't be in this room. This isn't a GenEd course." He pauses, making sure no one gets up to leave the room.

Reaching over with a tissue, Cody says under his breath, "Here, B, wipe the drool from your mouth."

"Oh shut up, Cody," I reply with a chuckle and a one finger salute. Because, yeah, I was totally staring and picturing Peters doing some "not safe for school" activities.

Why yes, Professor, I do need some extra help. Oh, meet in your office during office hours? See you then.

About the Author

Alexis Buxton is an avid reader turned author. A lover of all things love, Alexis enjoys reading all varieties of romance novels – the steamier, the better. Writing has always been a passion of hers and with the encouragement of friends and family, Alexis decided it was time to follow a childhood dream. She enjoys writing romance novels with damaged characters who need a little extra love and leave you *feeling all the feels*.

Born and raised in Ohio, Alexis currently resides in a small, lake town in Ohio with her husband and two small kiddos. Alexis is a small-town girl, through and through. When she doesn't have a book in her hand, you can find Alexis watching sports. She prides herself on being a Cleveland Browns fan, even on the hardest days (or years). She also enjoys adventures with her family, visiting breweries, attending races at her local dirt track, and supporting local businesses and restaurants.

Alexis runs on coffee, craft beers, and chaos, but she wouldn't have it any other way.

Stay in touch!
facebook.com/authoralexisbuxton
instagram.com/author_alexisbuxton
goodreads.com/alexisbuxton